Happy Housewarming
1986

Timid Virgins Make Dull Company

and Other Puzzles, Pitfalls, and Paradoxes

Also by Dr. Crypton

Dr. Crypton and His Problems:
Mind Benders from *SCIENCE DIGEST*

Dr. Crypton

Timid Virgins Make Dull Company

and Other Puzzles, Pitfalls, and Paradoxes

Viking

VIKING
Viking Penguin Inc., 40 West 23rd Street,
New York, New York 10010, U.S.A.
Penguin Books Ltd, Harmondsworth,
Middlesex, England
Penguin Books Australia Ltd, Ringwood,
Victoria, Australia
Penguin Books Canada Limited, 2801 John Street,
Markham, Ontario, Canada L3R 1B4
Penguin Books (N.Z.) Ltd, 182–190 Wairau Road,
Auckland 10, New Zealand

First published in 1984 by Viking Penguin Inc.
Published simultaneously in Canada

ISBN 0-670-71575-1
Library of Congress Catalog Card Number: 83-40680

The text of this book appeared originally, in different form, in *Science
Digest*.

Illustration on page 6 by Hal Aber, copyright © Hal Aber, 1982
Illustration on page 186 by Steven Henry, copyright © Steven Henry, 1983
Illustrations by Dan Murray and Anita Giraldo, copyright © Viking Penguin
Inc., 1984

Grateful acknowledgment is made to the following for permission to reprint
copyrighted material:

Cambridge University Press: A selection from *The Shakespearean Ciphers
Examined* by William and Elizabeth Friedman. Cambridge University Press,
1957.
Pulitzer Publishing Company: Crossword puzzle which appeared in the
December 21, 1913, issue of *The New York Sunday World*.

All of the limericks appearing in this book are reproduced by permission.

Printed in the United States of America
Set in Plantin

To Lora G. Huss

Contents

Introduction

I'm not sure Dr. Crypton would approve of my writing this introduction, but he left me little choice. Three days ago he plopped an incomplete manuscript on my desk and departed precipitously for a year of self-imposed isolation. As his secretary as well as his friend, I could not in good conscience submit the manuscript to the publisher in a fragmented form—I had to append an introduction.

If he had not left on such short notice, I would have been able to show him the day's correspondence, some of which he might have added to this volume. An aspiring enigmatologist in New York City sent him a 165-page palindromic manuscript, *Dr. Awkward & Olson in Oslo,* the length of which is 18,009 words. The story gets off to a promising start ("Tacit, I hate gas, aroma of evil") and ends with—you guessed it—"live foam, or a sage Tahiti cat." No doubt Dr. Crypton will want me to confirm that the entire story really is a palindrome.

A writer-artist team, united not only by their work but also by the vows of holy matrimony, submitted part of an illustrated novel that makes use only of words spelled with the letters *q, w, e, r, t, y, u, i, o* and *p,* the first row of alphabetic keys on the typewriter. Naturally, the protagonist's name is Qwerty.

The phobic reader may already have guessed why Dr. Crypton left for the year, and it's not because 1984 has Orwellian reverberations. It's because Dr. Crypton, in spite of his rational facade, suffers from an incurable disease, triskaidekaphobia, which is as difficult to live with as it is to pronounce. In 1984 the numerological forces of evil have conspired to serve up three Friday the thirteenths, in January, April and July. (Triskaidekaphobes who are not also plagued by mathephobia are urged to prove that three is the maximum number of times that Friday can fall on the thirteenth in a given calendar year.)

Consequently, at the stroke of midnight, when the multitudes of humanity who are numerologically deficient were toasting the New Year, kissing strangers and having their pockets picked in Times Square, the brilliant doctor fled into the night. A year in isolation may be good for him, however. Free of distraction, he can tackle the thorniest paradoxes. I know he is on the verge of answering the central question in the mathematics of morality: "If two wrongs don't make a right, is there a number n such that n wrongs do?"

I should really use this unexpected forum to demystify Dr. Crypton. Many people assume that his name is a pseudonym and write long letters speculating on his real identity. Isaac Asimov insists that the doctor's name comes from the Greek *kryptos*, meaning hidden (the Greek k becoming a c in Latin and, therefore, in English). The true explanation is much simpler. The doctor's name comes from that of his parents, Arnold and Sadie Crypton.

Dr. Crypton has transformed our vision of the world in perhaps as fundamental a way as Freud and Einstein. He discovered that words have a primary role in the fabric of the universe. Like other intellectual visionaries, he made this discovery at a very young age. And serendipity lent a hand.

As a child, Crypton was unusually happy. Unlike most other children in privileged families, he was allowed to dine with his parents. Often his father would wolf down his breakfast and rush out the door, exclaiming, "I have to go make a train." Crypton was proud of his father. After all, he thought, his father must be awfully strong to make trains for a living.

Young Crypton was in seventh heaven until one morning he discovered brother and sister wasps copulating in his sandbox. Traumatized by the primal scene, Crypton developed a sharp pain in what he called his thorax.

When he overheard his parents refer to him as a problem child, he knew that his calling was puzzles. Disturbed by their son's behavior, Arnold and Sadie consulted a baby doctor, who was speechless but cried a lot at their sad story.

In desperation, they sent Crypton to a child psychiatrist. Expectations were high because the boy immediately took to the games in the therapist's playroom. In the very first session he reported a dream in which his mother pointedly told him, "Two are better than one." (This dream, incidentally, was the focus of a recent international symposium, "Breast Envy and the Problem Child.")

After this promising start, things turned sour. In an inspired moment of free association, it occurred to young Crypton that *therapist* is an anagram of THE RAPIST. He promptly abandoned therapy.

His mental health, however, did not deteriorate. In fact, the pain in his thorax subsided when he realized that *incest* is an anagram of INSECT.

After that discovery, Crypton jumbled the letters in every word he came across. He refused to accept presents at Christmas because *Santa* is an anagram of SATAN. He promised himself he'd never take a wife because *marriage* is an anagram of A GRIM ERA. And he became active in the nuclear disarmament movement when he realized that *atom bombs* is an anagram of A MOB'S TOMB.

Suffice it to say that as an adult Crypton did much historical research into the importance of anagrams and other forms of wordplay—or, I should say, word seriousness. The results of his research are contained in this work.

Lora G. Huss,
Executive Secretary,
Institute of Paradoxology

January 4, 1984

Timid
Virgins
Make
Dull
Company

and Other Puzzles,
Pitfalls, and Paradoxes

1

The Topology of Cowlicks, Maelstroms and Russian Homes

Lora was determined to teach me how to spell the 1,185-letter name of the protein bovine glutamate dehydrogenase.* After I

```
*ACETYLSERYLTYROSYLSERYLISOLEUCYLTHREONYLSERYLPROLYLSERYL -
GLUTAMINYLPHENYLALANYLVALYLPHENYLALANYLLEUCYLSERYLSERYLV -
ALYLTRYPTOPHYLALANYLASPARTYLPROLYLISOLEUCYLGLUTAMYLLEUCY -
LLEUCYLASPARAGINYLVALYLCYSTEINYLTHREONYLSERYLSERYLLEUCY -
LGLYCYLASPARAGINYLGLUTAMINYLPHENYLALANYLGLUTAMINYLTHRE -
ONYLGLUTAMINYLGLUTAMINYLALANYLARGINYLTHREONYLTHREONY -
LGLUTAMINYLVALYLGLUTAMINYLGLUTAMINYLPHENYLALANYLSERY -
LGLUTAMINYLVALYLTRYPTOPHYLLYSYLPROLYLPHENYLALANYLPROLY -
LGLUTAMINYLSERYLTHREONYLVALYLARGINYLPHENYLALANYLPROLY -
LGLYCYLASPARTYLVALYLTYROSYLLYSYLVALYLTYROSYLARGINYLTY -
ROSYLASPARAGINYLALANYLVALYLLEUCYLASPARTYLPROLYLLEUCYLI -
SOLEUCYLTHREONYLALANYLLEUCYLLEUCYLGLYCYLTHREONYLPHENY -
LALANYLASPARTYLTHREONYLARGINYLASPARAGINYLARGINYLISOLEUCY -
LISOLEUCYLGLUTAMYLVALYLGLUTAMYLASPARAGINYLGLUTAMINY -
LGLUTAMINYLSERYLPROLYLTHREONYLTHREONYLALANYLGLUTAMY -
LTHREONYLLEUCYLASPARTYLALANYLTHREONYLARGINYLARGINYLVALY -
LASPARTYLASPARTYLALANYLTHREONYLVALYLALANYLISOLEUCYLAR -
GINYLSERYLALANYLASPARAGINYLISOLEUCYLASPARAGINYLLEUCYLVALY -
LASPARAGINYLGLUTAMYLLEUCYLVALYLARGINYLGLYCYLTHREONY -
LGLYCYLLEUCYLTYROSYLASPARAGINYLGLUTAMINYLASPARAGINY -
LTHREONYLPHENYLALANYLGLUTAMYLSERYLMETHIONYLSERYLGLYCY -
LLEUCYLVALYLTRYPTOPHYLTHREONYLSERYLALANYLPROLYLALANY -
LSERINE
```

committed the first three letters to memory, we took a cappuccino break in the spacious rec room of the Institute of Paradoxology.

"Crypy," Lora cooed, as she patted my head, "you would
look much more enigmatic if you got rid of the whorl in your
hair."

My windpipe engorged a mouthful of cappuccino. When I
finished gagging, I told her, "That's like saying space travel
would be more fun if we made the rockets go faster than the
speed of light."

"Huh? I don't follow you."

"It's really quite simple, Lora, Just as the laws of physics
indicate that we cannot make a rocket—or anything else—
move superluminally, the laws of mathematics indicate that I
cannot get rid of my whorl."

"Is that so?" Lora said. She reached deep into her handbag
and pulled out a left-handed pair of scissors.

"No, Lora, you're not going to cut my hair. Granted, you
could get rid of the whorl that way. What I mean is that the
gods of mathematics have decreed that a *full*, continuously
flowing head of hair must include a whorl. According to the
same decree, Lora, if you stir the cup of cappuccino in front of
you any way you like, as long as the surface of the coffee is not
disrupted, one point will always be stationary. In other words,
the whole surface cannot be in motion at once." I spent the
rest of the day elaborating on what I meant.

Such diverse phenomena as a whorl of human hair, the
swirling surface of a cup of coffee, a crumpled sheet of paper,
the wind on the surface of the earth, a stretched string, a
rubber disk, three gravitationally interacting planets and certain economic models are all governed by a powerful statement
in topology known as the fixed-point theorem. Topology is the
study of geometric properties that endure bending, stretching,
shrinking and other distortions. The fixed-point theorem,
which was proved before World War I by the Dutch math-

ematician Luitzen Egbertus Jan Brouwer, states that when a surface is subjected to certain forms of continuous distortion, at least one point of the surface will remain "fixed," or stationary. Put in this dry, abstract way, the theorem may not seem remarkable, but it has many impressive consequences for the physical world.

The validity of the fixed-point theorem can best be seen in a one-dimensional example: a string that is stretched in a straight line (diagram 1-1). Each point in the unstretched string (top horizontal line) corresponds to one and only one point in the stretched string (bottom horizontal line); matter, after all, can be neither created nor destroyed in this context.

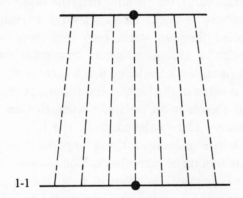

1-1

The dashed lines, which link points on the unstretched string with the same points on the stretched string, at first run in a northeasterly direction but ultimately go toward the northwest. This change in slope means that at some intermediate position a dashed line is perpendicular to the two strings. The perpendicular line corresponds to a fixed point. A similar argument reveals that the fixed-point theorem holds for a two-dimensional stretchable object, such as an elastic disk.

In the privacy of your own home, you can experiment with an amazing application of the fixed-point theorem. Take two identical sheets of graph paper and number the squares so that you can keep track of them. Next, crumple one of the sheets in any way you like, so long as it is not torn. Then lay the crumpled sheet on top of its uncrumpled twin in such a way that it does not protrude beyond the twin's edges. *Voilà!* No matter how you arrange the crumpled sheet, one of the squares will overlap (at least partly) its counterpart on the uncrumpled sheet. In the area of overlap there is a fixed point.

The fixed-point theorem also applies to spheres, such as the human head and the earth. It states that a sphere cannot be associated with a continuous field of radiating lines without there being a fixed point. For a full head of hair this means that there must be a fixed point, or whorl, from which the hair radiates. For the earth this means that the wind cannot be blowing everywhere at once; there is always a tranquil spot.

The fixed-point theorem states only that there is a fixed point; it provides no clue as to where that point may be located. Nevertheless, the knowledge that a point remains in the same position is often of the highest significance. Consider, for example, three objects in an isolated system that are interacting gravitationally. The mathematics of the interaction is so complex that it has generally proved impossible to write an equation for the motion of each object. The analysis of a three-body system is important, however, in such areas of physics as planetary astronomy. An astrophysicist might want to know whether three planetary bodies in isolation could exist in a stable arrangement in which each body orbited the other two. Such an arrangement is, in essence, the multidimensional equivalent of a fixed point. "Can a point remained fixed under certain forms of distortion?" is mathematically the same question as "Can a system of orbits remain fixed under the distorting influence of gravity?" The answer to both of these questions is an unequivocal "Yes!"

Economists have also relied on the fixed-point theorem. An economic model may contain a large number of algebraic equations, each of which includes many variables that corre-

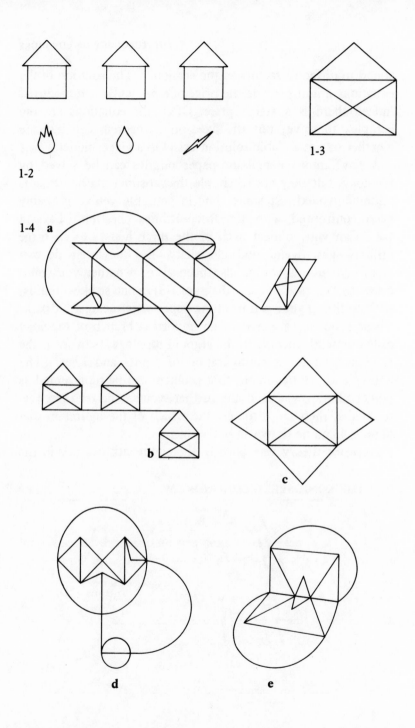

1-2

1-3

1-4 a

b

c

d

e

spond to different factors in the economy. The solution of the equations might provide the price of a particular commodity if indeed there is a stable price. Often the equations are too complex to solve, but the fixed-point theorem can indicate whether or not a stable solution exists in a given model.

A few famous pencil-and-paper puzzles can be solved by topology, but they are so simple that abstract mathematics is seldom invoked. At some time in your life you've probably been confronted with the three-utilities chestnut (diagram 1-2). Can you connect each of the three houses to all three utilities—gas, water and electricity—by lines that do not cross? No doubt you've also been asked whether you could draw the "crossed house" (diagram 1-3) in one stroke—that is, without lifting your pen from the paper or retracing your path. These problems are part of an important branch of topology called network theory. In the argot of topology, network is the general term for a configuration of points and lines. (The houses and utilities in the first problem can be represented as points.) Before you read any further, you should try these two problems, then try to determine which of the figures in diagram 1-4 can be drawn in one stroke.

Network theory was born in the eighteenth century in the

1-5

THE KÖNIGSBERG CONUNDRUM

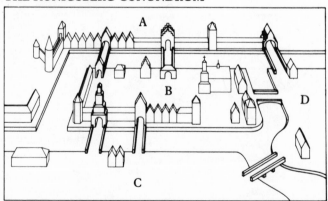

East Prussian city of Königsberg, now the Soviet town of Kaliningrad. The center of Königsberg was the island of Kneiphof in the Pregel River (diagram 1-5). Seven bridges connected Kneiphof, a neighboring island and the banks of the Pregel. The residents of Königsberg liked to go on long constitutionals—in keeping with the practice of a native son, the peripatetic philosopher Immanuel Kant. They wondered whether they could take a round-trip stroll across *all* seven bridges without crossing any bridge more than once. By enumerating the finite number of possibilities and examining them one by one, it is easy to see that it is impossible to take such a walk.

In 1736 the twenty-nine-year-old mathematical genius Leonhard Euler (pronounced "oiler") proved topologically that the round-trip journey was impossible. Moreover, he formulated and solved the general problem: "Given any configuration of the river and the branches into which it may divide, as well as any number of bridges, determine whether or not it is possible to cross each bridge exactly once." Born in Basel, Euler still has a place in history as the leading scientist of Swiss extraction. He made fundamental contributions to a wide variety of areas of mathematics, including topology, geometry, algebra, number theory, differential equations, the calculus of variations and the theory of geodesics. Euler was also concerned with the practical side of mathematics. To this end, he developed mathematical methods for studying cometary orbits, solar parallax, fluid flow and the motion of gases. The father of thirteen children, Euler was prolific in more ways than one: his collected works would fill eighty volumes, and he is said to have "dashed off memoirs in the half-hour between the first and second calls to dinner."

Euler's solution of the Königsberg bridge problem is a rare example of a proof in higher mathematics that is easy to follow. He introduced capital letters, *A*, *B*, *C* and *D*, to represent masses of land that were kept apart from one another by the river (diagram 1-6). If a traveler crossed a bridge from area

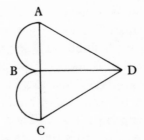

1-6

A to area B, Euler would indicate this by the notation AB. If the person then went from area B to area C, this would be expressed by the combination BC; the entire journey would be denoted by the sequence ABC. (From here on, such a sequence will be called a journey sequence.) In the case of two bridges that connected the same masses of land—say, A and B—the notation would not distinguish between the bridges, because they were equivalent for purposes of the walk. Nevertheless, because there were two bridges, the combination AB (or BA) would appear twice in the journey sequence. Euler reduced the map of Königsberg to its topological essence: a network in which each point represents a landmass and each line a bridge.

Suppose the number of bridges leading to a given area of land—say, W—is an odd number. (This was the case for each of the four land areas in Königsberg.) I will use the letters W, X and Y here because I'm referring to land areas in general and not to the ones specifically labeled in the diagrams. How many times will W appear in the journey sequence? Give this a try before you read on. Well, if there is only one bridge to W, W will appear only once, regardless of whether the traveler uses the bridge to leave W or to reach it. Suppose there are three bridges. If the traveler starts at area W, W will appear twice because a sequence such as WXWY exhausts the three bridges. By the same token, if he starts elsewhere, W will still appear twice because a sequence such as YWXW also uses up the three bridges. Similar reasoning will show that if there are five bridges, the letter W will appear three times in the journey sequence. To put it all together, for an odd number of bridges—call the number m—W will appear in the sequence $\frac{1}{2}(m + 1)$ times.

In Königsberg there were five bridges to Kneiphof (B), three bridges to the other island (D), three bridges to one bank of the Pregel (A) and three bridges to the other bank (C). Now, according to the preceding analysis, B will appear three times in the journey sequence, D two times, A two times and C two times. In other words, the journey sequence will contain nine letters. This result, however, leads to a contradiction. A nine-letter journey sequence represents eight bridges because each pair of letters in a string of nine letters represents a trip across one bridge. There are only seven bridges in Königsberg, and so a stroll that exhausts all the bridges is impossible unless one bridge is crossed more than once.

Note that at no point in Euler's analysis does he mention the round-trip nature of the stroll. He simply proved that it is impossible to stroll across all the bridges without repeating one, regardless of where one starts and finishes.

Before you read beyond this sentence, you might pause to tackle the general problem of an arbitrary number of bridges and an arbitrary number of landmasses. Euler proved that a nonoverlapping stroll can be taken only when there are either zero or two points (land areas) from which emerge an odd number of lines (bridges). In the latter case, the trip must begin at one of these two points and end at the other.

The result bears directly on the pencil-and-paper puzzles because taking a nonoverlapping stroll is equivalent to drawing a closed figure in one stroke; in both cases the object is to visit prescribed destinations without retracing your steps. In the crossed house there are exactly two points associated with an odd number of lines; hence, according to Euler's proof, the figure can be drawn with one stroke (presuming one starts at one of these points). The proof is also relevant to the three-utilities chestnut. If it were possible to connect the three houses to the three utilities in the required way, each house and each utility would have three lines emerging from it. The fact that each of the six points would be associated with an odd number of lines means that the connection is impossible. Now that you know Euler's proof, you will be able to amaze people by deciding at a glance whether or not a given closed figure can be drawn in one stroke without retracing. Go back and apply the proof to the figures in diagram 1-4.

Of course, knowing that a particular figure can be drawn in principle doesn't mean that you can draw it in practice. I have already told you that when there are two points associated with an odd number of lines, you must begin at one of them. Euler had another good suggestion: When two regions are connected by two bridges, the bridges should be ignored in the first analysis; in other words, the route should be traced across the remaining bridges. The nature of the route will not change substantially when the bridges that were ignored are reinstated. For example, the "roof" of the crossed house can be disregarded at first because, in effect, it is two bridges that link the top left point of the house with the top right point. That reduces the house to the configuration in diagram 1-7. Armed with the knowledge that one must start at either the bottom left or the bottom right (because those are the two points from which an odd number of lines emerges), it is an easy matter to trace the figure (diagram 1-8). With the roof restored, one starts as before, pauses to take a side trip to complete the roof and then finishes up as before (diagram 1-9).

Euler's results apply only to figures that are traced on certain surfaces, such as one side of a sheet of paper. Everything changes when the surface is more complex. Consider the object that topologists call a torus but which we know to be a doughnut. The problem of the three utilities can be solved on the surface of a torus. Try it. The solution is shown in diagram 1-10.

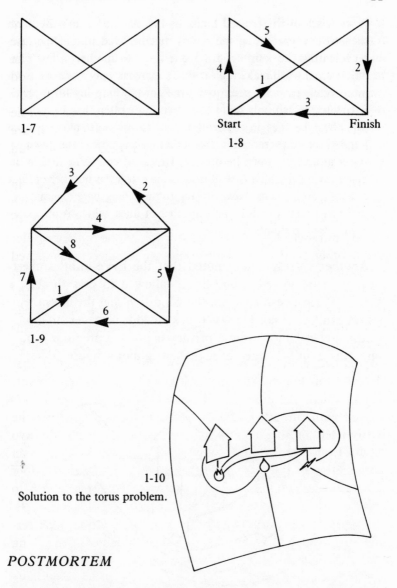

1-7

1-8

1-9

1-10

Solution to the torus problem.

POSTMORTEM

Two readers sent me amusing letters after the piece on which this chapter is based appeared in *Science Digest*. G. W. Jukes, of British Columbia, wrote:

If we think of the crossed house as the plan of a man's life, with the points representing the towns that he lived in and the lines representing the journeys from one town to another, a few minutes' thought will make it clear that a man can only leave one town more often than he goes to it (the town where his life began). Likewise, he can only go to one town more often than he leaves it (the town he dies in). Therefore, all towns must have an even number of lines radiating from them except two, the town he starts in and the town he dies in. Unless of course he dies in his home town, in which case all towns have an even number of lines radiating from them. Now turning to the Königsberg diagram, we find three points with an odd number of lines, which is obviously an impossible situation.

Another correspondent noted that the three-utilities chestnut could be solved if one line is allowed to pass through a house (which doesn't violate the condition that the lines themselves cannot cross). He was quick to add, however, that only in the Soviet Union, where privacy is not at a premium, could one run a utility line through a neighbor's house (diagram 1-11).

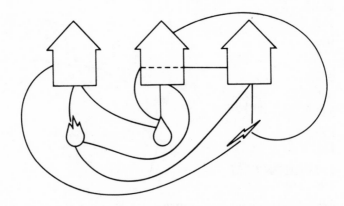

1-11

2

The SAT Snafu:
The Schoolboys Who Beat
the College Board

Of all geometric figures, the circle is the simplest and the most benign. The simplicity is captured by a concise mathematical definition, which even mathephobes will understand: the set of all points in a plane that are equidistant from a given point in that plane. The circle is benign because it is soft and round and has no sharp corners on which you might get caught. Indeed, it has no corners at all.

The circle, however, also has a sinister side. Consider two problems. The first concerns two quarters that are side by side with George looking left (diagram 2-1). If the quarter on the left is rolled along the quarter on the right until it reaches the position of the question mark, where will George be gazing? Do this in your mind's eye rather than with real quarters.

The second problem is more fanciful (diagram 2-2). Suppose a long piece of string were looped around the earth along the equator and tied tightly in a circle. Forget about mountains and valleys and picture the earth as a perfect sphere. Now, imagine that the loop is cut and a piece of string only six feet

2-1

long is inserted, and a new loop around the earth is formed. If you try to pull the loop away from the surface of the earth, how far can you pull it? (In other words, how much slack is there?)

Did you decide that George would be upside-down and that the loop would still be hugging the earth's surface because six more feet of string are negligible compared with the earth's circumference (which, of course, is the length of the original string)? Both these answers are commonly given, but they are both dead wrong.

George will actually end up looking to the left, and the loop of string can be positioned so that it is nearly a foot off the earth's surface at every point. With the quarters you can convince yourself of the correct answer by setting up the problem on a table and rolling the left-hand coin.

The looped earth requires much more analysis. Imagine that the earth is not a sphere but a cube (diagram 2-3). In that case the loop of string forms a square. If the string is lengthened by six feet, it can be oriented as in diagram 2-4, where each hollow segment of string corresponds to three feet. Sure enough, the top horizontal piece of string is three feet off the earth's surface. If you pulled up on the horizontal length so that the portion of the string that overhangs the earth assumed the shape of a triangle, the apex of the triangle would be even

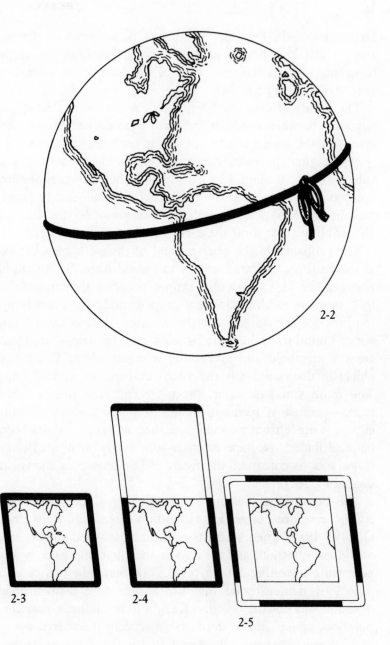

2-2

2-3

2-4

2-5

farther away. In fact, the string can be arranged so that at every point it is always at least nine inches from the earth (diagram 2-5). In this case each of the hollow line segments corresponds to nine inches.

The beauty of diagram 2-5 is that it works for an "earth" of any size. In other words, if the earth were the size of, say, the universe, the string would still be at least nine inches away!

My original problem concerned not a cubic earth but a spherical one. It should be evident that the two situations are analogous. I leave it to the mathematically minded to prove that in the spherical equivalent of diagram 2-5 the loop is almost always a foot off the earth's surface.

The problems of the quarters and of the earth are what we at the Institute of Paradoxology call mind traps. This term is reserved for any apparently simple situation that run-of-the mill, intuitive thinking does not properly address. A mind trap requires deep, imaginative analysis. Often, the more you think about a mind trap, the more paradoxical it becomes—until you cross a threshold and everything is crystal clear. The paper object in diagram 2-6 is the visual analogue of a mind trap. The more you look at it, the more confused you may become—because it seems to be an "impossible shape." Actually, it is made from a rectangular sheet of paper that has been cut and folded. No tape or other adhesive is involved. I challenge you to construct the figure. (The answer is shown in diagram 2-16.)

The Educational Testing Service (ETS), which administers college entrance exams, has fallen into three mind traps since October 1980, when students were first provided with copies of the test questions and the answer sheet in compliance with a new truth-in-testing law in New York State. In two cases a schoolboy demonstrated that the answer to a mathematical question was not the one that ETS, a $150-million-a-year corporation, chose. In the third case a student discovered a second correct answer. I urge you to try the three questions,

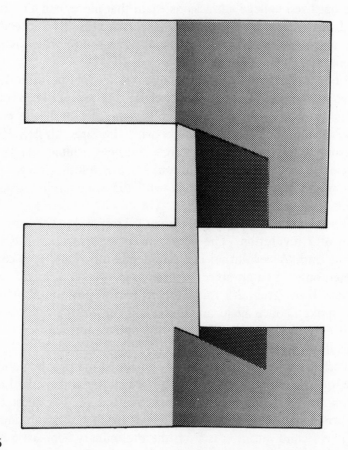

2-6

The figure in the illustration is made from one rectangular sheet of paper that has been folded and cut. No tape or any other adhesive is involved. I challenge you to construct the figure.

reprinted in "College Admissions Test" in diagram 2-7, before you read further.

The first question was on the Scholastic Aptitude Test, the standardized college admissions exam that more than a million high-school juniors and seniors take each year. ETS intended the answer to be (B) 3. The actual answer is 4, which is not even among the choices!

Look at diagram 2-8. The small circle starts at position A. (I have put a spoke on the small circle so that you can keep track of its orientation in space as it rolls along; notice that in position A the spoke is in contact with the large circle.) ETS reasoned that as the small circle journeys around the large circle, it makes three revolutions—one revolution each time the spoke reestablishes contact with the large circle (at positions C, E and A).

These positions, however, do not correspond to the completion of a revolution. The very concept of a revolution is the mind trap. A revolution is a 360-degree turn, and it is completed only when an object returns to its original spatial orientation. In diagram 2-8 this happens first at position B, where the spoke is once again horizontal and runs to the right. Now it is easy to comprehend where the four revolutions are completed (B, D, F and A).

Perhaps you now realize why I included the problem about the quarters. The two problems are quite similar. In both cases an unexpected revolution is involved. (If the quarter is returned to its starting point, it will make *two* revolutions.)

The second question is from the Preliminary Scholastic Aptitude Test, which is a warm-up for the SAT and a screening exam for the National Merit Scholarships. The intended answer was seven. ETS thought that the problem was a simple one and reasoned as follows: Considered separately, the pyramids have a total of nine faces. When put together in the prescribed way, the resulting solid has seven faces (two of the original ones having been lost to the interior of the solid).

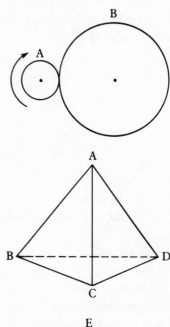

1. In the figure, the radius of circle *A* is ⅓ the radius of circle *B*. Starting from the position shown in the figure, circle *A* rolls around circle *B*. At the end of how many revolutions of circle *A* will the center of circle *A* first reach its starting point?
(A) ⅔ (B) 3 (C) 6 (D) 9/2 (E) 9

2. In pyramids *ABCD* and *EFGHI* shown at right, all faces except base *FGHI* are equilateral triangles of equal size. If face *ABD* is placed on face *EFG* so that the vertices of the triangles coincide, how many exposed faces will the resulting solid have?
(A) Five   (B) Six   (C) Seven
(D) Eight   (E) Nine

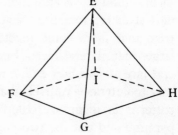

3. Which row contains both the square of an integer and the cube of a *different* integer?
(A) 7, 2, 5, 4, 6   (B) 3, 8, 6, 9, 7
(C) 5, 4, 3, 8, 2   (D) 9, 5, 7, 3, 6
(E) 5, 6, 3, 7, 4

DO NOT GO ON TO THE NEXT
SECTION UNTIL INSTRUCTED TO
DO SO.

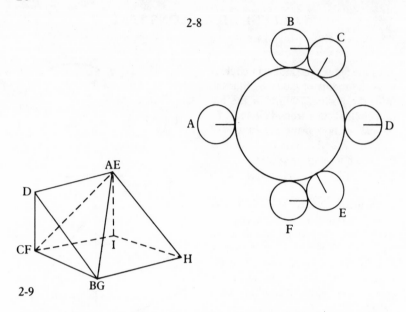

2-8

2-9

A seventeen-year-old schoolboy in Florida realized that the question was a mind trap. He conjured up the resultant solid in his mind's eye and counted the number of faces. He saw only five! He visualized that, in two cases, two of the original triangular faces come together in the same plane to form a large quadrilateral face. (Look at diagram 2-9. One quadrilateral face is *D-AE-H-BG;* the other is *D-AE-I-CF.*) The best way to convince yourself that this is true is to cut out the two patterns in diagram 2-10, fold and glue each one to form a pyramid and put the two together.

When I first read the second test question, I came up with yet another answer: eight. I imagined the four-sided pyramid *inside* the five-sided pyramid, so that triangle *ABC* is flush against triangle *EFG* (diagram 2-11). I realized that the four-sided pyramid would not be completely swallowed up but would poke through the five-sided pyramid at vertex *D*. The resulting solid indeed has eight faces. (In mathematics, unlike in life, "solids" are allowed to fit inside each other.)

a

b

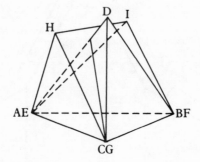

2-11

Lora thinks the answer to the test question is six. She reasoned in the same way as the folks at ETS, but also thought that a third face of the original nine doesn't count, because if the pyramids were real objects a face would be resting on a surface, such as a tabletop, and thus would not be "exposed," as the problem delineates.

The intended answer to the third problem was (B) because 9 is the square of 3 and 8 is the cube of 2. Choice (C) was designed to trick students who reasoned that 4 is the square of 2 and that 8 is the cube of 2 but who didn't recognize that two 2s do not satisfy the "different integers" requirement. Nevertheless, choice (C) is as correct as choice (B) because 4 is also the square of negative 2, which most certainly is a different integer from positive 2. It is amusing that ETS slipped into this particular trap because the commercial courses that prepare students to take the SAT—courses that ETS frowns on—always caution to be on the lookout for negative numbers.

POSTMORTEM

ETS is not always on the receiving end of mind traps; it occasionally dishes them out, too. A high-school junior sent me a problem from the booklet *Taking the SAT*, which ETS issues. He could not understand how the answer to the following problem could be anything but (C) 4:

In diagram 2-12, what is the greatest number of nonoverlapping regions into which the shaded region can be divided with exactly two straight lines?

(A) 6   (B) 5   (C) 4   (D) 3   (E) 2

He sent me two configurations (diagrams 2-13 and 2-14) to justify his choice of (C) 4. The answer is actually (B) 5, the solution ETS had in mind. The correct configuration is shown in diagram 2-15. The ETS booklet indicates that only 7 percent of students answer the question correctly.

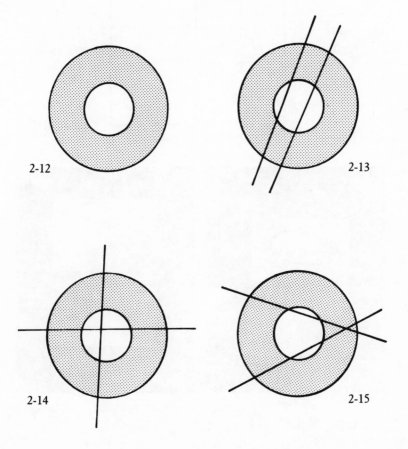

"IMPOSSIBLE SHAPE"

The perplexing paper configuration in diagram 2-6 can be made by three cuts, a lengthwise fold and a 180-degree twist (diagram 2-16).

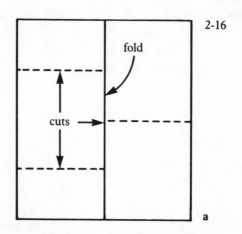

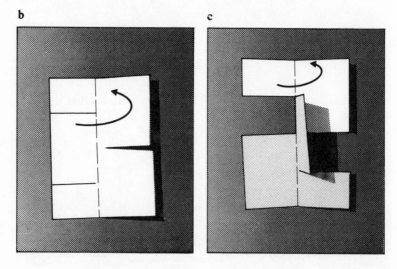

3

The Dead-Twin Studies and the Case for Prenatal Psychotherapy

For twenty-eight years an obscure scholarly journal whose logo includes a trash can has reported on innovative solutions to age-old problems in science. The nature-nurture controversy has been resolved in favor of nurture, the journal says, by means of a series of experiments known as the dead-twin studies. A battery of psychometric tests was given to identical twins, one of whom had been dead since birth. In all skill areas the living twin performed better than his dead sibling. In fact, the dead twin showed no performance at all. Since the twins have the same genetic makeup, the difference in skill levels can be entirely attributed to how the living twin was reared.

Another article in the journal suggests that the chance of making serendipitous discoveries in medicine would be greatly increased by eliminating all bias through a triple-blind test, in which "the subject does not know what he is getting, the nurse doesn't know what she is giving and the investigator doesn't know what he is doing." The article continues: "Half-

way through the experiment, randomization is increased by a
process known as turnabout—the patient administers the drug
to the investigator, and the results are evaluated by a student
nurse."

Yet another article calls attention to the inheritance pattern
of death, which has been overlooked because "genetics has
historically been a pragmatic and arbitrary branch of medicine, as would any field whose origin stems from a lonely and
celibate monk staring vacuously at pea pods in a monastery
courtyard."

The latest psychotherapies are also covered in this remarkable journal. An abstract entitled "Prenatal Psychoanalysis: A
New Approach to Primary Prevention in Psychiatry" evaluates
the therapeutic effect of intensive psychoanalysis on third-
trimester fetuses. A follow-up study was conducted when the
fetuses had matured into adults of age thirty. The chief measure of normal adult adjustment was an annual salary of at
least $36,000. The abstract hinted that the therapy might be
ineffective if the fetus itself did not pay for the treatment.

The name of this eclectic quartley is *The Journal of Irreproducible Results*, the official organ of the Illinois-based Society for Basic Irreproducible Results. Founded in 1955 by
Alexander Kohn, an Israeli biophysicist, the journal is essen-
tially a humor magazine, to which scientists of every stripe
contribute. The aim of the journal is not only to elicit yucks
but also to blow the whistle, through clever satire, on the kind
of experimental gibberish and sloppy thinking that all too
often makes its way into prestigious scientific publications.
(Subscriptions are available from P.O. Box 234, Chicago
Heights, Illinois 60411.)

The most often-discussed article is a piece by George H.
Kaub entitled *"National Geographic*, the Doomsday Machine," which appeared in 1974. The upshot of the piece is
that "publication and distribution of *National Geographic*

magazine must be immediately stopped at all costs!" The reason is simple. No one ever throws out the magazine. Back issues gather dust in basements, attics, garages, libraries and thrift shops. Kaub warns that eventually the accumulated issues will depress North America to the point where the sea inundates the continent.

A rebuttal by L. M. Jones of the University of Georgia disputes Kaub's calaculations. According to Jones's math, if the National Geographic Society continues to publish twelve issues of the magazine each year, it will take 24.92×10^9 years before enough issues accumulate to depress the continental landmass a mere 100 feet. "Since this length of time is several times greater than the present age of the Earth," Jones concludes, "it should be obvious that we or future generations have little to fear from the National Geographic Society."

Another piece, by Victor Milstein, takes issue with Jones's analysis because it is based on the faulty assumption that the circulation of the magazine is evenly distributed over the forty-eight contiguous states. In point of fact, the distribution is weighted toward the densest population centers, namely the East Coast and the West Coast. Milstein concludes that these coastal areas will fall below sea level in a mere 457.247×3^7 years, while the central part of the United States will be elevated an average of 217 meters.

Skimming through back issues of the journal, I came across such intriguing articles as "Reading Education for Zoo Animals: A Critical Need" and "Seasonal Egg-Scattering Behavior in *Leapus paschalis*, the Easter Bunny." But the journal is funniest when it quotes, à la *The New Yorker*, titles and passages from legitimate scientific publications. No made-up titles could draw more guffaws than the following real ones: "Direct Measurements of Thermal Responses of Nude Resting Men in Dry Environments" (*European Journal of Physiology*, 1968); "Psychotic Visitors to the White House" (*American Journal of*

Psychiatry, 1965); "Use of Telephone Interviews in a Longitudinal Fertility Study" (*The Public Opinion Quarterly*, 1964); "An Instance of the Pitfalls Prevalent in Graveyard Research" (*Biometrics*, 1963) and "Maternal Behavior in the Domestic Cock under the Influence of Alcohol" (*Science*, May 12, 1967).

Of all the passages quoted, the biggest sidesplitter is from the *San Francisco Chronicle* for April 6, 1973: "A plastic plug inserted into a man's sperm duct seems to hold 'tremendous promise' of future reversible vasectomies, a George Washington University urologist reported here yesterday. Dr. Fletcher C. Derrek said there is no reason to be discouraged even though all thirteen of the first volunteer patients seem to have become permanently sterile. 'I suspect it's just a matter of perfecting technique,' said Derrek."

Another ribald passage noted by the journal also found its way into the pages of *The New Yorker*. The passage is from the *Leominster* (Massachusetts) *Daily Express:* "The proceeds will be used to purchase Hi-Lo beds for the hospital. These beds are constructed so they can be manually raised to accommodate both patients and nurses."

In my own reading, I have found that if an article has a silly title, the joke seldom stops there. Witness the piece "Why Is Mrs. Thatcher Interrupted So Often?" in the December 23–30, 1982, issue of the stuffy and renowned British journal *Nature*. The abstract accompanying the article reads:

If a conversation is to proceed smoothly, the participants have to take turns to speak. Studies of conversation have shown that there are signals which speakers give to inform listeners that they are willing to hand over the conversational turn. When one speaker interrupts another, the two can be said to be disputing who has the turn. Interruptions can occur because one participant tries to dominate or disrupt the conversation. But it could also be the case that mistakes occur in the way these subtle turn-yielding signals are transmitted and received. We demonstrate that many interruptions in an interview with Mrs. Margaret Thatcher, the British Prime Minister, occur at points where independent judges agree that her turn appears to have finished. It is suggested that she is unconsciously displaying turn-yielding cues at certain inappropriate points.

One can only hope that British scientists will not let their fascination with Mrs. Thatcher and the royal family (I can see a journal article now: "The Toilet Training of Prince William") divert them from traditional areas of research.

Meanwhile, on this side of the Atlantic, scientists have more important concerns. Under the headline DEAD PEOPLE MORE LIKELY TO BE BURIED, the May 9, 1983, issue of *Medical World News* reported that the government released a $180,000 study entitled "Morbidity and Health Care Utilization." In the words of the forty-page study:

> Regression analysis was used to explain variation in utilization measures (doctor visits, hospital admissions, and hospital days) associated with a set of socioeconomic and morbidity indicators. The results supported the hypothesis that variation in utilization rates between socioeconomic groups is strongly connected to health status. . . . Individuals in poor health were almost seven times as frequent users of physician services as those in excellent health and spent an average of 21 times as many days in the hospital.

A dependable source for reports on research of similar import is *Psychology Today*, where a feature story once reported that psychologists have concluded that vacations are good for us.

I have found that even the most revered publications slip up occasionally. At *Scientific American* it is the policy of the editors to write every caption so that it ends flush right—in other words, the last line must be completely filled. Moreover, if the caption spans a full page, it is broken into two banks, each containing the same number of lines. To meet these constraints, it is often necessary for the editors to pad a caption with trivial information. This practice works as long as the information is correct, but under the pressure of deadlines, gremlins can slip in.

An opening illustration for "Skin Transplants and the Hamster," in the January 1963 issue of *Scientific American*, shows a hamster whose cheek pouches have been stretched full of cotton wool, in the interest of science. The caption, which is split into two banks, ends on the following note: "The hamster's parsimonious habits are the source of its common name: *hamstern* in German means 'to store or to hoard.' " Do you detect something fishy? (The word *fish*, incidentally, comes from the word *fishy*, because the aquatic vertebrates are known the world over for their questionable behavior.) Two months later, *Scientific American* published a letter from an incredulous reader: "Is a wolf called 'wolf' because he wolfs his food? Or a fox 'fox' because he's foxy?"

I know of science editor at a major weekly news magazine who put together a story on the structure of galaxies. To illustrate spiral structure, he chose the Andromeda nebula, and gave the art director a spectacular shot of the nebula that he wanted to run with the article. "Pretty nice," the art director said. "I think the concept is good, but the composition would be better if we photographed the nebula from the other side."

Scientists themselves often resort to humor to point out the limitations of their discipline. More than one statistician has told his students the following joke, which confirms the old adage that figures can't lie but liars can figure. Two college freshmen were bragging about their high schools. "Twenty-five percent of my class are going to college," said the first frosh. "That's nothing," said the other. "Fifty percent of my class enrolled. Would have been one hundred percent, only the other guy had to go to work."

In the field of artificial intelligence, which has been heralded by Wall Street and the news media with fanfare befitting the Second Coming, self-deprecating humor has the salutary effect of deflating overblown expectations. Isaac Asimov told me about a mathematician who was studying the numbers spewing out of a high-speed computer. "My God," he said. "It would take two hundred mathematicians five thousand years to make a mistake this big."

It is said that adjacent to the main-frame computer in the basement of Argonne National Laboratory, a particle-accelerator center in Chicago, is a transparent case labeled IN CASE OF EMERGENCY, BREAK GLASS. Inside the case is an abacus.

Science fiction does not have a monopoly on berserk computers such as HAL, the lip-reading paranoiac in the movie *2001: A Space Odyssey*, whose name is a one-letter shift of the letters IBM. Craziness was built into the first electronic computer, ENIAC, an acronym for Electronic Numerical Integrator and Computer. The mathematician John von Neumann upgraded the machine so that it would be suitable for the demanding work on the atomic bomb at Los Alamos. Von Neumann named the improved version Mathematical Analyzer, Numerical Integrator and Computer. Not all of his co-workers immediately recognized that the name yields the acronym MANIAC.

A subtle sense of humor was not typical of all of the scientists cooped up at Los Alamos. Apparently, the Nobel prize–winning theoretical physicist Richard Feynman amused himself by cracking the safes in which blueprints of the bomb were stored and leaving guess-who notes for the guards.

Feynman's humor also permeates his writing. In a broadside against the "new math" curriculum in elementary schools, Feynman ridiculed its preoccupation with the "precision" provided by the language of mathematical sets. "A zookeeper, instructing his assistant to take the sick lizards out of the cage, could say, 'Take the set of animals which is the intersection of the set of lizards with the set of sick animals out of the cage.'

This language is correct, precise set theoretical language, but it says no more than 'Take the sick lizards out of the cage.' "

The use of humor for rhetorical purposes is, of course, not unique to the sciences. But science writing, particularly in the field of mathematics, exhibits a special kind of humor, best described as obscure and concealed, that can be found elsewhere only in the works of such wordplayful novelists as Vladimir Nabokov. An extreme example is the 1923 text *Invariantentheorie*, by the Austrian mathematician Roland Weitzenböck. Somewhere along the line, one of his readers discovered that the foreword is an acrostic, based on the first letter of each sentence. The letters spell *"Nieder mit den Franzosen!"* ("Down with the French!").

For some inexplicable reason, mathematicians often slip jokes into the indexes to their books. The popular text *Calculus and Analytical Geometry* includes the unusual entry "Whales." When I first noticed this, I immediately flipped to the corresponding page. Again and again I read the page, but I could find no mention of whales. It finally dawned on me that the page contained a graph in the shape of a whale's back.

A potshot at the concept of self-reference in mathematical logic is buried deep in the index to Joseph Rotman's *The Theory of Groups: An Introduction*. Before I describe the potshot, I want to say a word about self-reference. In 1918 Bertrand Russell introduced the now-famous paradox of the Barber of Seville, who is instructed to shave all and only those men who do not shave themselves. The paradox rears its ugly head in the question: "Who shaves the barber?" According to his instructions, if he does not shave himself, then he must shave himself; but if he shaves himself, then he must not shave himself. Russell concocted this paradox as an easy-to-appreciate analogue of a problem in mathematical set theory that troubled him: a class of objects is defined by the objects it contains, but the objects in turn are defined by their belonging to the class.

The swipe at self-reference in the index to *The Theory of Groups: An Introduction* begins with the curious entry "Pipik, Moshe. See Navel, Maurice." But under "Navel, Maurice," it says "See Pipik, Moshe." To appreciate the joke, you must know that *pipik* is Yiddish for belly button. Note how obscure the humor is. You must first stumble on one of the entries in the index, bother to consult the cross-reference, know what *pipik* means and understand that self-reference was once a large thorn in the side of mathematics.

Jokes designed for the cognoscenti also abound in the life sciences. Biologists have plenty of opportunities for obscure humor in the names they give to the thousands of new plants and animals that are discovered each year. According to the taxonomic system devised by the eighteenth-century Swedish botanist Carl von Linné, each plant and animal is classified by two Latin names, one for the genus and one for the species. (So enraptured was Linné by this nomenclature that he changed his own name by Latinizing it, to become Carolus Linnaeus.) In an article in *BioScience*, Ralph Lewin of the Scripps Institution of Oceanography lists some of the weird names he's encountered: "*Diogenes rotundus* (an alga found living in a barrel), *Pockockiella papenfussii* (a seaweed named after two eminent South African phycologists), *Hummbrella hydra* (a parasol-shaped alga named by Sylvia Earle in honor of Professor Humm), *Saprospira toviformis* (so called because it gyres and gimbles), and *Didemnum ginantonicum* (named in honor of Lou Eldredge's favorite beverage)." Nevertheless, the ultimate joke in biological nomenclature, Lewin notes, may have been Linnaeus's *Homo sapiens* ("thinking man").

4

Was Shakespeare a Playwright?
The History of the Anagram

The name of William Shakespeare can be anagrammed in more ways than one, to reveal much about the playwright. He is universally admired (witness the anagram WE ALL MAKE HIS PRAISE), and he is generally considered the greatest English writer of all time (I ASK ME, HAS WILL A PEER?). In spite of Shakespeare's titanic reputation, a group of scholars known as anti-Stratfordians believe he was a fraud. More than four thousand books and articles have been published that claim Shakespeare was the pen name of an Elizabethan luminary who wanted to write plays anonymously. Seventeen candidates have been proposed, the strongest being Francis Bacon, the British empiricist philosopher who served in the court of James I.

In the 1890s the question of who wrote Shakespeare's works was one of the hottest intellectual issues around. Learned men and women debated it over dinner, much as we might discuss nuclear proliferation today. No one ever doubted that there

was an actor from Stratford-upon-Avon named William Shakespeare. The issue was whether he could have written great
drama. The actor Shakespeare had no more than a grammar-
school education in a small, rural English town. Could this
hick have written erudite plays that draw heavily on
knowledge of the law, royal custom, world history, classical
languages and ancient literature? Bacon had command of all of
these subjects, and so he has been advanced as the real Shakespeare the playwright.

Ironically, it is the anagram that has helped call into question Shakespeare's authorship. The anti-Stratfordians have
pointed to anagrams and other cryptograms in Shakespeare's
plays that they insist are cryptic signatures of the real author.
Nevertheless, all these cryptic signatures are illusions, as William and Elizabeth Friedman demonstrated in their brilliant
book *Shakespearean Ciphers Examined.*

I am fascinated by the debate over Shakespeare's authorship
because it is an outstanding example of how easy it is for
well-intentioned but self-deluded fanatics to misuse the principles of an entire branch of science, in this case cryptography,
the science of making and breaking codes.

The word *anagram* comes from the Greek *anagrammatizein,*
meaning to transpose letters. The first person who earned a
living by scrambling words was Lycophron, a Greek tragedian
of the third century B.C. who was hired by the pharaoh of
Egypt to create amusing anagrams of the names of his courtiers. From the pharaoh's name in Greek, Lycophron came up
with MADE OF HONEY, and he jumbled the queen's name to get
PURPLE FLOWER.

In the Middle Ages, Jewish mystics, the cabalists, exten-
sively investigated scrambled writing. They found that in
Hebrew *Noah* is an anagram of GRACE and that *Messiah* is an
anagram of HE SHALL REJOICE. At the trial of Jesus, Pontius
Pilate had asked, *"Quid est veritas?"* ("What is truth?"). The
cabalists realized that Jesus could have responded with the

question's anagram: "EST VIR QUI ADEST" ("It is the man who is here").

The anagram, like the riddle, has had its share of fatal consequences. When André Pujom, a seventeenth-century Frenchman, discovered that his name was an anagram of PENDU À RIOM ("hanged at Riom"—in anagramming, *i* and *j* are interchangeable, as are *u* and *v*), he saw to it that this omen was fulfilled. He promptly committed a murder, for which he was eventually caught and sentenced to death by hanging at Riom, the center for the administration of justice in the region of Auvergne.

Anagrams, albeit imperfect ones, have also figured in English jurisprudence. In 1634, one Eleanor Davies told the High Commission that she could see into the future like the Biblical Daniel because her name was an anagram of REVEAL O DANIEL! The judge pointed out that she had incorrectly anagrammed her name. If she had been more observant, he admonished, she would have noticed that the letters in *Dame Eleanor Davies* can be scrambled to form NEVER SO MAD A LADIE. But the judge was wrong, too, because his anagrammatical effort was short an *e*.

More recently, an unintended anagram kept at least one man from winning the most hare-raising treasure hunt in history. In the lavishly illustrated book *Masquerade*, author-artist Kit Williams planted clues to the whereabouts of an 18-carat cottontail that he had buried somewhere in England. For thirty months the bounty bunny eluded two million treasure seekers the world over. One ardent treasure hunter wrote to Williams that he knew he could find the hare if only he discovered Williams's real name. *Kit Williams*, he wrote, had to be a pseudonym because it is an anagram of I WILL MASK IT.

The French developed such a passion for jumbling words that Louis XIII created the position of Anagrammist to the King. The most famous of all anagrams is the pseudonym of an eighteenth-century French writer whose given name was

François Marie Arouet. The nom de plume comes from jumbling the letters in *Arouet, l.j.*, where *l.j.* stands for *le jeune,* "the younger." What is the pseudonym? Why, none other than **VOLTAIRE**.

The anagram has also played a role in American history. Thomas Jefferson's answer to British and French curbs on American shipping was the extreme Embargo Act, which prohibited ships engaged in international trade from entering or leaving American ports. The act was nicknamed **O-GRAB-ME** (an anagram of *embargo*) because many ships openly violated the act, defying the government to "grab" them in order to force compliance. *O-Grab-Me* is actually *embargo* spelled backward. Lewis Carroll coined the term *semordnilap*—the word *palindromes* in reverse—for this kind of anagram.

The *New York Journal*, a Hearst newspaper, once faked an obituary for a certain Reflipe W. Thanuz because it suspected the rival paper, the *New York World*, of lifting its copy. Sure enough, the *World* ran the obit, too, prompting the *Journal* to point out that **REFLIPE W.** is an anagram of *we pilfer* and that **THANUZ** is the phonetic pronounciation of *the news*. The *World* retaliated by slipping the name Lister A. Raah into a story. After the *Journal* picked up the story, the *World* announced that *Lister A. Raah* is an anagram of **HEARST A LIAR**.

Anagrams have even reached the Soviet Union. Ninel Kulagina was a noted Soviet parapsychologist in the late 1960s and early 1970s. (In this country the *Saturday Review* featured a picture of her levitating a Ping-Pong ball, with "biological luminescence" emanating from her eyes.) Kulagina chose *Ninel* for a stage name because it is the semordnilap of **LENIN**.

Anagrams have also served scientific purposes. In the seventeenth century it was not uncommon for an astronomer to record a discovery anagrammatically while he searched for confirming data. That way, he could establish priority in a discovery without having to announce it prematurely. Christian Huygens, the Dutch mathematician and astronomer, sent

a friend an apparently witless anagram—AAAAAAACCCCCD
EEEEEGHIIIIIIILLLLLMMNNNNNNNNNNOOOOPPQRRSTTTTTUUUUU—
that concealed a major discovery. Do you know what it was?
Huygens had discovered the shape of Saturn's rings. The anagram disguised the statement *Annulo cingitur tenui plano, nus-
quam cohaerente, ad eclipticam inclinato* ("It is girdled by a thin
flat ring, nowhere touching, inclined to the ecliptic").

The anagram Galileo concocted for his discovery that Venus
has phases like those of the moon was more than just a string
of letters in alphabetical order. The anagram, HAEC IMMATURA
A ME JAM FRUSTRA LEGUNTUR, O.Y., would make perfect sense
in Latin if it were not for the meaningless *O.Y.* stuck on the
end. Minus the *O.Y.*, the sentences translates: "These unripe
things are now read by me in vain." (If Galileo had spoken
Yiddish, he would have dropped the periods in *O.Y.* to form
oy, a cry of lament that would have been quite appropriate at
the end of the translated sentence.) Galileo's sentence could be
jumbled to read: CYNTHIAE FIGURAS AEMULATUR MATER
AMORUM. The meaning is poetic: "The phases of Cynthia
[goddess of the moon] are imitated by the Mother of Love
[Venus]."

The period in history when Shakespeare wrote has been
called the Golden Age of Anagrams. All the best people,
even Queen Elizabeth, scrambled words. Anagramming had
become such a consuming passion in both England and
France by the late seventeenth century that the poet John
Dryden called for an end to the "torturing of one poor
word ten thousand ways." In a satirical piece by Joseph
Addison, the eighteenth-century English essayist and poet, a
word-conscious lover goes into seclusion in order to construct anagrams of his sweetheart's name. Six months later
he emerges, only to discover that he misspelled her name in
the first place.

The word scramblers defended themselves against ridicule
by proudly observing that the virtue of jumbled wordplay is

Ffrauncis Bacon
or tribute or giuing

the praise of the worthiest —
the praise of the worthiest affection
the praise of the worthiest power
the praise of the worthiest person

a

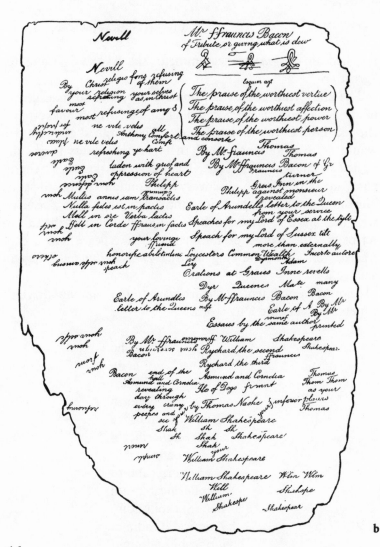

Newill

Mr ffrauncis Bacon
of Tribute or giving what is dew

Nevill

By Christ religio fons refusing
of them
your religion your selves
refreshing as in Christ
most favour
most refusinge of amy s
ne vile velis
Anthony Comfort all
ne vile velis Comp
refreshing ye hart
laden with grief and
oppression of heart
Philipp
Multis annis iam transactis
Nulla fides est in pactis
Mell in ore Verba lactis
Hell in Corde ffraus in factis
your loving
Friend
honorificabilitudini
peach

The praise of the worthiest vertue
The praise of the worthiest affection
The praise of the worthiest power
The praise of the worthiest person
and consorte
By Mr fraūncis Thomas
By Mr ffrauncis Bacon of Gr
Frauncis
turner
Greis Inne in the
Philipp against monsieur
revealed
Earle of Arundells letter to the Queen
from your service
Speaches for my Lord of Essex at the tylt
Speach for my Lord of Sussex tilt
more than externally
Leycesters Common Wealth Incerto autore
Ley Bynneman Adam
Orations at Graies Inne revells

Dyr Queenes Mate many
Earle of Arundlis By Mr ffrauncis Bacon Bacon
letter to the Queens mᵗ Earle of A By Mr
By Mr
Essaies by the same author printed

By Mr ffrauncis reveff William Shakespeare
Bacon vish Rychard the second Shakespear.
ffrauncis
Rychard the third
Bacon end of the Asmund and Cornelia
Asmund and Cornelia hall Thomas
revealing Ile of Dogs frmnt Thom Thom
day through as your
every cranny by Thomas Nashe inferior plaiers
peepes and your Thomas
see William Shakespeare
Shak sh sh
Sh Shak sh
Shakespeare
Shak
your
William Shakespeare

William Shakespeare Wm Wm
Will Shakspe
William Shakespe
Shakspe Shakespear

b

4-1

To the left is a facsimile of the cover of the Northumberland Manuscript, a key document in attempts to show that William Shakespeare
was the pen name of Francis Bacon, the celebrated philosopher. This
manuscript may have been written by one of Bacon's scribes. The cover
has on it the names of Shakespeare and Bacon and a version of the long
nonsense word that Shakespeare used in *Love's Labour's Lost*. Above is a
legible version of the cover.

revealed in *anagrams* anagrammed: ARS MAGNA is Latin for "great art."

The anti-Stratfordians got much anagrammatic mileage out of the long word *honorificabilitudinitatibus,* which Shakespeare slipped into *Love's Labour's Lost.* They argued that no one would coin a nonsense word that peculiar unless it was designed to conceal a message. Their case was greatly strengthened in 1867 by the discovery in London of the so-called Northumberland Manuscript, the scribblings of a scrivener who may have worked for Bacon. On the cover of the manuscript are the names of Bacon and Shakespeare and a contracted version of the long word, *honorificabilitudini* (diagram 4-1).

Another document, which was found among Bacon's papers, dissects the long word:

ho

hono

honori

honorifi

honorifica

honorificabi

honorificabili

honorificabilitu

honorificabilitudi

honorificabilitudini

honorificabilitudinita

honorificabilitudinitati

honorificabilitudinitatibus

The above diagram, if it was actually conceived by Bacon, suggests that he examined each and every syllable in the long word. To anagram a word, one must indeed carefully analyze its internal structure; however, one would be inclined to look not at syllables but at individual letters.

Armed with a connection between Bacon, Shakespeare and the long word, the anti-Stratfordians devoted themselves to discovering its cryptic significance. In the pages of the journal *Baconiana*, the long word and the contracted form are anagrammed in no less than seven ways (four in Latin and three in English) that purportedly reveal Bacon's authorship. Before you read further, I urge you to have a go at unscrambling the long word. Remember that you may interchange *i* and *j* as well as *u* and *v*.

The seven anagrams are as follows, with translations given for the Latin:

1. HI LUDI, F. BACONIS NATI, TUITI ORBI ("These plays, F. Bacon's, are preserved for the world").
2. ABI. INIVIT F. BACON. HISTRIO LUDIT ("Begone. F. Bacon has entered. The actor is playing").
3. INITIO HI LUDI FR. BACONO ("These plays, in the inception, Francis Bacon's").
4. HI LUDI, TUITI SIBI, FR. BACONO NATI ("These plays, produced by Francis Bacon, guarded for themselves").
5. FAIR VISION, BACON BUILT IT, HID IT.
6. BUT THUS I TOLD FRANIIIIII BACON.
7. BUT THUS I TOLD FRAN!!!!!! BACON.

It should come as no surprise that a word as long as twenty-seven letters yields numerous anagrams. This fact alone is sufficient reason to abandon the project of finding a unique cryptic signature. The purpose of cryptography is not only to conceal a message but to do so in an unambiguous way, so that a person who knows the key can decipher it. Bacon, who was a top-notch cryptographer, would undoubtedly have chosen a sophisticated cipher system that was not open to more than one interpretation. In 1910, when Sir Edwin Durning-Lawrence published the first anagram on the above list, he claimed it was the only intelligible anagram of the long word and offered 100 guineas ($500) to anyone who could prove otherwise. He was to pay the money to a Mr. Beevor, who submitted the second anagram on the list.

The fact that the remaining anagrams are extremely contrived is even more damaging. The third has no verb. Moreover, it is not a true anagram of the contracted version of the long word; an *o* should be an *i*. The fourth anagram is so barbaric that it could not have been penned by Bacon, who wrote entire books in flawless, graceful Latin. Moreover, it makes little sense—for what could it possibly mean, the Friedmans ask in *Shakespearean Ciphers*, for plays to "guard themselves"? The fifth anagram is grammatically peculiar as well as convoluted. The sixth required an amusingly apologetic explanatory note when it was cited in the November 1893 issue of *Baconiana:* "In a cypher or an anagram I should expect to find Francis spelled Franiiiiii, 'Fran-six,' pronounced 'Fran-sis,' that is, 'Francis.' " The concocter of the seventh anagram avoided the problem by turning the *i*'s upside-down to form exclamation marks!

In evaluating the authenticity of a cryptic signature, one should consider what the cryptographer does. He starts with the message he wants to encipher; then he selects a code and applies it to the message in order to transform it into a cover text. Since the cryptographer begins with the message, it should be perfectly intelligible and free of grammatical peculiarities. Would one be likely to start with a message as bizarre as "Fair vision, Bacon built it, hid it"? Certainly not. One would probably encrypt a message along the lines of "I, Francis Bacon, wrote these plays." Alas, no statement like that has ever been squeezed out of the long word.

If the above is not enough to dispose of the long word, a look at its history is. The word could not have been coined by Bacon, because it was first used in print three hundred years before he was born! Dante, for one, used it at the end of the thirteenth century. (The gullible will make much of the fact that the long word is an anagram of UBI ITALICUS IBI DANTI HONOR FIT—"Where there is an Italian, there honor is paid to Dante.") By the sixteenth century, *honorificabilitudinitatibus* seems to have become a popular nonsense word, much as *supercalifragilisticexpialidocious* is today.

In 1903 Walter Begley, a British clergyman, called attention to the closing lines of the epilogue to *The Tempest:*

As you from crimes would pardon'd be
Let your indulgence set me free.

Begley anagrammed the lines to reveal an astonishing message:

TEMPEST OF FRANCIS BACON, LORD VERULAM,
DO YE NE'ER DIVULGE ME YE WORDS.

Although James I had given Bacon the title Baron Verulam, the message is invalid, the Friedmans observed, because it contains one more *a* than the text does.

The fundamental weakness of the anagrammatic method is that a lengthy text generally can be anagrammed in more ways than one. The Friedmans claimed to have come up with two true anagrams of *The Tempest* lines. The first suggests that Shakespeare was the nom de plume of Samuel Clemens, who usually preferred to write under the name Mark Twain:

R[EAD]R: BELIEVE IT OR NOT, MY RUDE
PLAY WAS CODED FOR FUN. GOD SAVE ME,
CLEMENS

Cryptic signatures aside, it is worth noting that Clemens was an anti-Stratfordian. The other anagram supports Shakespeare's claim to authorship:

I WROTE EVERY LINE MYSELF. PURSUE NO CODE.
E. TOLD ME BACON'S A G.D. FRAUD.

My secretary, Lora G. Huss, who may have special insights into such matters because her name is an anagram for the way she looks, was not convinced by the Friedmans' efforts. She noticed that neither of their examples is a true anagram. The first has an extra *a*, like Begley's flawed effort. The second has an extra *a*, too, and an *m* and an *r* are missing. Lora spent the better part of an afternoon studying the lines in question. To my delight, she discovered a definitive anagram that puts the other versions to shame:

F.B., YOU FRAUD, MULL EERIE CODE.
I, DR. CRYPTON, AM LONG-ESTEEMED W.S.
NO RUSE.

AFTERTHOUGHT

Shakespeare himself has not avoided the charge of having left his cipher signature in works that are not usually attributed to him, such as the King James Version of the Bible. The psalms in the King James Version are so melodic that scholars think they had to have been translated into English by a master poet. Try to find Shakespeare's cipher signature in Psalm 46:

God is our refuge and strength, a very present help in trouble.

Therefore will not we fear, though the earth be removed, and though the mountains be carried into the midst of the sea;

Though the waters thereof roar and be troubled, though the mountains shake with the swelling thereof. Selah.

There is a river, the streams whereof shall make glad the city of God, the holy place of the tabernacles of the most High.

God is in the midst of her; she shall not be moved: God shall help her, and that right early.

The heathen raged, the kingdoms were moved: he uttered his voice, the earth melted.

The LORD of hosts is with us; the God of Jacob is our refuge. Selah.

Come, behold the works of the LORD, what desolations he hath made in the earth.

He maketh wars to cease unto the end of the earth; he breaketh the bow, and cutteth the spear in sunder; he burneth the chariot in the fire.

Be still, and know that I am God: I will be exalted among the heathen, I will be exalted in the earth.

The LORD of hosts is with us; the God of Jacob is our refuge. Selah.

In this psalm—the forty-sixth—the forty-sixth word is *shake* and the forty-sixth word from the end (discounting *Selah*, which means "amen") is *spear*. The King James Version was published in early 1610, when Shakespeare was forty-six. The number 46 is made up of two 23s, and indeed there were two important 23s in Shakespeare's life: his birthday is tradition-ally celebrated on April 23 and he died on April 23.

Robert Anton Wilson, author of *Illuminatus* and *Schro-dinger's Cat*, made much of the number 23 in his article "Mere Concidence?" in the January 1982 issue of *Science Digest*. He rattled off a whole slew of bizarre coincidences, many of them involving literary figures. The following anecdote captures the flavor of the whole piece: "Novelist William Burroughs, while living in Tangier in 1958, had a conversation with a Captain Clark, who mentioned that he had been sailing 23 years with-out an accident. That day, Captain Clark had his first serious accident. In the evening, while thinking about this, Burroughs flipped on the radio and heard a bulletin about a crash of an airliner. The flight number was 23 and the pilot was also a Captain Clark." Wilson then suggests that such wildly im-probable incidents are not accidental but are indicative of some underlying order in nature that has been ignored by establishment scientists.

Being on the lookout for uncanny coincidences in life is not unlike searching for cryptic signatures in Shakespeare. Life is so rich that, from time to time, events are bound to be bizarrely juxtaposed. By the same token, Shakespeare was so prolific that somewhere in his writing there must be isolated phrases that when anagrammed or otherwise decoded could be taken for cryptic signatures. Indeed, in life and in Shakespeare it would be eerie if one did *not* find seemingly eerie correlations.

I want to share with you my reply to Wilson, which appeared in *Science Digest:*

Much too much is often made of the uncanniness of rare events. For every Dame Rebecca West whose servants find a hedgehog in the garden while she happens to be writing a story about such a discovery, there are scores of novelists whose stories do not play themselves out in reality as they are being written. For every Freud or Jung who hears a poltergeist while discussing extrasensory perception, there are undoubtedly numerous people who discuss parapsychology without concurrently experiencing paranormal phenomena.

In each of these cases, if you could count the number of "bizarre" episodes and the number of "normal" episodes, I am convinced you would find that they obey the laws of probability. If the odds against an event are a billion to one, the event can still happen. Indeed, you would *expect* to observe the event—at an average rate of one event for every billion nonevents.

In other cases, the odds can be precisely calculated, and these calculations should undermine any feelings of uncanniness caused by rare events. From time to time you've probably come across a short newspaper item describing someone who was dealt a bridge hand of 13 cards of one suit. You should not react by groveling in awe at the power of the card gods.

The odds of being dealt all the cards of a suit are 158,753,-389,899 to 1. In *A Mathematician's Miscellany,* J. E. Littlewood points out that roughly 2 million Englishmen play an average of 30 hands of bridge a week; that's 3,120,000,000 bridge hands a year. If you add in the bridge hands that the rest of the world is playing, it is not surprising that you've heard of someone being dealt an entire suit.

Another source of eerie coincidences is shared birthdays. Surely you've been in a situation in which a small group of people compared birthdays and found, to their surprise, that at least two of them were born on the same day of the same month. Suppose there are ten people in the group. Intuition may suggest that the odds of two sharing a birthday are quite poor. Probability theory, however, shows the odds are better than one in nine.

If you like to win bets, you should keep in mind that for a group of 23 people the odds are in favor of at least two of them sharing a birthday. (For 22 people, the odds are slightly against this.) Warren Weaver, the celebrated mathematician who wrote *Lady Luck: The Theory of Probability*, once explained these odds at a dinner party of Army and Navy officers. The group included 22 people, and one proposed that they test Weaver's explanation. "We got all around the table without a duplicate birthday," Weaver recalled. "At which point a waitress remarked, 'Excuse me. But I am the twenty-third person in the room, and my birthday is May 17, just like the general's over there.' "

This all goes to show that you need look no further than probability theory in order to understand the mundaneness of coincidences.

No sooner was the above rebuttal published than several readers pointed out that I had slipped up in an amusing way. Do you see what they had noticed?

In replying to Wilson, whose favorite coincidences concern the number 23, I had cited the paradox of shared birthdays, in which the number 23 has a special status. And in the anecdote I told about Weaver, it is the twenty-third person who saves the day. But by my own admission, it would be uncanny if people did not, on occasion, unwittingly hang themselves in uncanny ways.

5
Writing High on the Hog: The Acrostic as Cryptogram

If Francis Bacon, the celebrated philosopher, classical scholar, distinguished barrister, amateur cryptographer and member of the court of James I, wrote the plays attributed to Shakespeare, why didn't he do so under his real name? The anti-Stratfordians say Bacon used a pseudonym because his aristocratic contemporaries, in spite of their professed love of the theater, considered play-writing a vulgar craft. A racier explanation is that Bacon was the secret illegitimate son of Queen Elizabeth. Unbeknownst to Mom, he discovered his royal lineage and contrived to get revenge on her for not acknowledging him by writing pseudonymous plays that expose the seamier side of royalty. According to this theory, Bacon wrote *Hamlet* as a warning to his mother, the Queen.

But why the nom de plume William Shakespeare? The failure of Baconians to find in the plays even one clear instance of Bacon's anagrammatic signature led them to analyze the purported pseudonym itself. There the Baconians also failed, and so they tried to anagram versions of Shakespeare's name in which *W.* or *Mr.* was substituted for *William*.

One overly zealous Baconian, Benjamin Haworth-Booth,

concentrated on the phrase *Maister William Shakespeare* because he noticed that *Maister* appeared before Shakespeare's
name in the dedication of a poem written by two of the
Bard's contemporaries, Francis Beaumont and John Fletcher.
Haworth-Booth placed great importance on the dedication
because the names of the authors conjoined by the word *and*
could be jumbled by substituting *i* for *j* to form the telling
message: TRUE HAM FLITCHES AND NO FINER BACON. Since
ham is a close cousin of bacon, Haworth-Booth apparently
saw the anagram as pointing two fingers at Francis Bacon.

Try your mind at finding the real playwright's anagrammatic signature in the words *Maister William Shakespeare*.
Haworth-Booth brought home the bacon with the revealing
anagram I MASKE AS A WRITER. I SPELLE HAM. What a wit, that
Bacon!

To bolster his case, Haworth-Booth went whole hog in
searching for other concealed porcine references. In the Latin
platitude *acceptam refero* ("That which is referred to is accepted"), which appeared on the title page of several Elizabethan works, he found the anagram MEE A FAT PORCCER. The
peculiar spelling of *mee*, he explained, was common then, and
"as there is no *K* in Latin, the double *C* is cleverly utilized
instead." In another work he discovered the anagram I FRY IN
STEWD SUET.

Fortunately for the Baconians they had other arguments to
fall back on in order to demonstrate that their man used the
pseudonym Shakespeare. Bacon once wrote: "The greatest
matters were often carried in the weakest ciphers." He must
have had in mind, among other things, the military code of
Julius Caesar. Caesar simply replaced each letter with the one
that followed it by three places in the alphabet. The Baconians, of course, read much more into Bacon's words and
searched for other cryptograms in Shakespeare's plays. Besides
the anagram, the acrostic was the simplest cryptogram that the
Baconians pursued.

An acrostic is a passage in which letters at designated intervals spell out a word or phrase that somehow relates to the passage. Like *anagram*, the word is of Greek origin. A familiar kind of acrostic is the acronym, which is based on the first letter of each word. The early Christians adopted the fish as a symbol of Christ because the Greek word for *fish* is an acronym of "Jesus Christ, Son Of God, Savior." The English word *cabal*, although it may have come from the Hebrew, was first widely used during the reign of Charles II (1660–85) because the word was an acronym of the names of his five scheming ministers: Clifford, Ashley, Buckingham, Arlington and Lauderdale.

Perhaps there's a hidden, acronymic order to the world, as was first betrayed by my discovery that Sigmund Freud's last name stands for "First Revealed Erotic Universal Drives" and that *Darwin* is clearly an acronym for "Demonstrated Aryan Race Was Initially Neanderthal." In the bowels of the library at UCLA, I stumbled upon an obscure, revealing work, *Acrostic Dictionary: The Face Value of Words*, by the Reverend Isidore Myers. With a 1915 copyright ("Constituting Only Protection Yet Revealed, I Gladly Have This"), a dedication ("Deeming 'English' Delightful, I Congratulate And Thank Inventor Openly Now") and a foreword ("For Our Readers, Everywhere, With Our Respectful Duty"), the book unravels about a thousand acronyms. Look up *appendicitis* and you'll find "A Popular Pain Even Nowadays; Doctors Insist Cutting It, Though It's Stomachache." *Beaches*, of course, are "Best Endeared As Couples' Havens, Encouraging 'Smacks.' "

The overall tone of the dictionary is righteous. For example, *sin* is defined as "Stains Inmost Nature," *satisfy* as "Stop And Think, Impartially, Seriously, For Yourself" and *school* as "Strengthening Character Here—Object Of Life."

Many of the entries that are not moralistic are sex-linked, although they are designed to vex both genders. *Anomaly* is defined as "Answering 'No' Often Means A Lady's 'Yes' " and *male* as "Merely A Lady's Escort."

The acronym is only the simplest form of acrostic. Acrostics come in all shapes and sizes, and are limited only by human ingenuity in verbal high jinks. In the so-called simple acrostic, initial letters of lines spell out a word. As an added twist, the simple acrostic can be made alliterative by starting all the words in a line with the same letter. Of greater complexity is the progressive acrostic, whose message is formed from the first letter of the first line, the second letter of the second line, the third letter of the third line, and so on. Another kind of acrostic is the simple telestic, in which the message depends on the last letter of each line. Most remarkable is the progressive telestic, in which the message is spelled out from the last letter of the first line, the second-to-last letter of the second line, the third-to-last letter of the third line, and so on.

The writing of acrostics is obviously a painstaking process, but many eloquent ones are on record. Below are three famous examples: a simple acrostic that Lewis Carroll dedicated to his young friend Gertrude Chataway, a progressive acrostic that Edgar Allan Poe dedicated to the poet Frances Sargent Osgood, and an anonymous verse that is at once a simple acrostic and a simple telestic.

A SIMPLE ACROSTIC BY LEWIS CARROLL

Girt with a boyish garb for boyish task,
Eager she wields her spade: yet love as well
Rest on a friendly knee, intent to ask
The tale he loves to tell

Rude spirits of the seething outer strife,
Unmeet to read her pure and simple spright,
Deem, if you list, such hours a waste of life,
Empty of all delight!

Chat on, sweet Maid, and rescue from annoy
Hearts that by wiser talk are unbeguiled.
Ah, happy he who owns that tenderest joy,
The heart-love of a child!

Away, fond thoughts, and vex my soul no more!
Work claims my wakeful nights, my busy days—
Albeit bright memories of the sunlit shore
Yet haunt my dreaming gaze!

A PROGRESSIVE ACROSTIC BY EDGAR ALLAN POE

For her this rhyme is penned, whose luminous eyes,
Brightly expressive as the twins of Leda,
Shall find her own sweet name, that nestling lies
Upon the page, enwrapped from every reader.
Search narrowly the lines!—they hold a treasure
Divine—a talisman—an amulet
That must be worn at heart. Search well the measure—
The words—the syllables! Do not forget
The trivialest point, or you may lose your labor!
And yet there is in this no Gordian knot
Which one might not undo without a sabre,
If you could merely comprehend the plot.
Enwritten upon the leaf where now are peering
Eyes scintillating soul, there lie *perdus*
Three eloquent words oft uttered in the hearing
Of poets, by poets—as the name is a poet's, too.
Its letters, although naturally lying
Like the knight Pinto—Mendez Ferdinando—
Still form a synonym for Truth.— Cease trying!
You will not read the riddle, though you do the best you can do.

SIMPLE ACROSTIC AND TELESTIC BY AN ANONYMOUS ELIZABETHAN

Unite and untie are the same—so say you
Not in wedlock, I ween, has this unity been
In the drama of marriage, each wandering out
To a new face would fly—all except you and I
Each seeking to alter the spell in their scene.

A fellow enigmatologist, inspired by Poe's creation, sent me the following birthday greeting, which I leave to you to decipher should you want to know more about me.

Poe did it, so why not I!?
Gadzooks, why not better his muse?
You, a mench of infinite skills, immediately grasp the idea.
You'll have no trouble with my cyphering,
But this mere cleverness is not my only cause;
I say to you, Happy Birthday!
Hew! I'm afraid all wit now leaves my poetry,
And I put foolish garbage in to fill the spaces out,
A greater maven might still inject pith here,
But not I. Sparkling intelligence might have been my goal origi-
    nally,
Now I just want to get the job done. And so it is.

I urge you to discover the dual acrostic magic of the following verse that a Mrs. Harris contributed to the October 10, 1885, issue of *Golden Days:*

He squanders recklessly his cash
In cultivating a mustache;
A shameless fop is Mr. Dude,
Vain, shallow, fond of being viewed.
'Tis true that he is quite a swell—

A smile he has for every belle;
What time he has to spare from dress
Is taken up with foolishness—
A witless youth, whose feeble brain
Incites him off to chew his cane.
Leave dudes alone, nor ape their ways,
Male readers of these Golden Days.

The above verse is the best example I've found of an acrostic that sacrifices neither wit nor meter. The fourth letters of the lines spell out QUANTITATIVE and the last letters spell out HEEDLESSNESS.

All acrostics, no matter how simple or elaborate, have one thing in common. The letters that spell out the message are not distributed helter-skelter but are always positioned according to some preconceived order. Consider part of a speech by Cordelia, the daughter of the title character in Shakespeare's *King Lear:*

I yet beseech your majesty—
If for I want that glib and oily art,
To speak and purpose not, since what I well intend,
I'll do 't before I speak—that you make known
It is no vicious plot, murther, or foulness.

Yet no one in his right mind—except perhaps an obsessed Baconian—would take this haphazard arrangement for an acrostic signature. It works like this: the fifth letter of the first line, the eighth letter of the second line, the twenty-fourth letter of the third line, the fifth letter of the fourth line and fifth letter of the fifth line spell out BACON.

The acrostics pointed out by Baconians, however, are scarcely more compelling. In sixty-three years of issues of *Baconiana,* a journal devoted to showing that Shakespeare was

Bacon, only two acrostics have been offered that are not laugh-
able. The first is from *The Tempest:*

> Begun to tell me what I am; but stopp'd
> And left me to a bootless inquisition,
> Concluding "Stay: not yet."

The other is from *Much Ado About Nothing:*

> Then sigh not so,
> But let them go,
> And be you blithe and bonny,
> Converting all your sounds of woe
> Into hey nonny, nonny.

In both cases the acrostic has the form
> **B**
> **A**
> **Con.**

In the second case, however, the Baconians did something
that was not kosher. Without pointing out what they had
done, they broke in two the real first line ("Then sigh not so,
but let them go") in order to make the acrostic work! In any
event, the acrostic is undoubtedly accidental. No true acrostic
takes more than one letter from each line; **BACON** takes three.
Moreover, the name Bacon contains only five letters, and
fairly common ones at that, and so there is no reason to assume that its appearance is anything but accidental.

Trying to find Bacon's acrostic signature in the following
two passages from Shakespeare's plays is a good exercise in
convoluted thinking. The punctuation and spelling have been
left as they originally were so as not to sabotage any concealed
acrostic. The lines are numbered to indicate how they broke in
the original.

FROM THE TEMPEST:

(1) he hath no drowning marke vpon him, his complexion
(2) is perfect Gallowes; stand fast good Fate to his han-
(3) ging: make the rope of his destiny our cable, for our
(4) owne doth little aduantage. If he be not borne to be
(5) hang'd, our case is miserable.

FROM A WINTER'S TALE:

(1) As fat as tame things: one good deed, dying tonguelesse
(2) Slaughters a thousand, wayting vpon that.
(3) Our prayses are our wages: you may ride's
(4) With one soft kisse a thousand furlongs, ere.

Pigheaded Baconians have claimed that the passage from *The Tempest* conceals the acrostic HE IS HANG'D HOG (bacon, of course, being a hanged hog). The *he* and *is* come from the first words of the first two lines; the *hog* comes from the initial letters of the last three lines read from bottom to top, and the *hang'd* comes from the first word of the last line.

The passage from *A Winter's Tale* is supposed to hide the acrostic AS FAT AS SOW. The *as fat as* comes from the first line, and the *sow* comes from the initial letters of the remaining lines. Naturally, a fat sow would make good bacon; hence, the acrostic signature of Francis Bacon.

POSTMORTEM

Kip Kennedy, of Medford, Oklahoma, sent me the following letter about the version of this chapter that appeared in *Science Digest:* "After reading Dr. Crypton's article on whether or not Francis Bacon penned Shakespeare's plays, I found some of the evidence agreeable. But as I read it, I began to wonder if Bacon did not also pen the name Dr. Crypton and write the

[*Science Digest*] article from the grave." Kennedy then quoted my discussion of the flimsy acrostics in *The Tempest* and *Much Ado About Nothing* (the lines are broken as they were in *Science Digest*):

> In both cases the acrostic has the form
>
> B
>
> A
>
> Con.
>
> In the second case, however, they had to break the real first line in two to make the acrostic work.
>
> In any case, the acrostic is probably accidental. No true acrostic takes more than **one** letter from each line; *Bacon* takes three.

6

Death on King Four: Patricide, Suicide, Heart Failure and Mass Execution

Chess holds its master in its own bonds—fetters and in some ways shapes his spirit, so that under it the inner freedom of the very strongest must suffer.   —*Albert Einstein*

It is plain that the unconscious motive actuating the players is not the mere love of pugnacity characteristic of all competitive games, but the grimmer one of father-murder.   —*Ernest Jones*

The passion for playing chess is one of the most unaccountable in the world. It slaps the theory of natural selection in the face. It is the most absorbing of occupations, the least satisfying of desires, an aimless excrescence upon life. It annihilates a man. You have, let us say, a promising politician, a rising artist, that you wish to destroy. Dagger or bomb are archaic, clumsy and unreliable—but teach him, inoculate him with chess.   —*H. G. Wells*

Chess—the king of games and the game of kings—has always aroused intense passions in players and kibitzers alike. The Royal Game has recently been in the public eye in the form of the Canadian documentary *The Great Chess Movie* and of Walter Tevis's novel *The Queen's Gambit*. These two works, one of them nonfiction and the other fiction, provide an occasion for comparing chess in life with chess in literature.

The Great Chess Movie is a wonderful documentary about the monomaniacal world of high-level chess. You don't even have to know how a Knight moves in order to appreciate the insanity of the world that is unfolded in this hilarious film. One hears top-ranked grandmasters describe Anatoly Karpov, the reigning Soviet world champion, as "a Martian, but a very vulnerable and human Martian." With an enormous head attached to a corpse-frail body, Karpov is known in chess circles as "the Fetus." One gets the impression from the interview footage in *The Great Chess Movie* that most grandmasters are in a world of their own. In an interview at the time he was world champion and a household name, Bobby Fischer was asked what it meant to be Bobby Fischer. "I don't know. It's my name," he replied. And when asked who his favorite writers were, he said, "Uh, I don't know. I'm really mainly magazines" (Fischer really talks like that). Victor Korchnoi, the Soviet émigré who challenged Karpov for the world title, is seen explaining that his homeland should not regard him as a traitor: "I only betrayed how to move the Bishop and make better Pawn structure."

The world of master chess is so bizarre that novelists writing about the game have been hard pressed to concoct situations that are more fantastic than what actually happens. Mirco Czentovic, the idiot-savant champion in Stefan Zweig's 1944 novella *The Royal Game,* is not unlike the real-life Mir Malik Sultan Kahn, an illiterate Indian slave who somehow managed to master the magic of the sixty-four squares. An English diplomat purchased Kahn and brought him to Europe in 1928, where he played in tournaments and trounced strong grand-masters, including the world champion José Capablanca. At the peak of Kahn's career, the diplomat sent him back to India—and he was never heard from again.

The insanity of the chess world is exquisitely captured by Vladimir Nabokov's 1930 novel *The Defense*, in which the Soviet grandmaster Luzhin, who comes to see the world as a giant chess game, commits "sui-mate" (suicide) by jumping out a window. *The Defense* does not include chess problems, in the sense of positions that can be set up on a board. Surprisingly, however, Nabokov chose to end a book of poetry, *Poems and Problems*, with eighteen chess problems! Two of them are shown in diagram 6-1. The first is deceptively simple, and the solution to the second is ingenious.

6-1 **a**
VLADIMIR NABOKOV
White to mate in three.

6-1 **b**
VLADIMIR NABOKOV
White to take back his last move and mate in one.

Other writers, such as Isaac Asimov, have focused not on the bizarre behavior of chess masters but on the mechanical, analytical aspects of the game itself. In Asimov's story "Exit to Hell," a computer is deciding whether a man who accidentally damaged life-sustaining equipment should be punished by being exiled to outer space—a punishment worse than death. One technician has programmed the case for the prosecution, and another the case for the defense. The two men mechanically play a game of chess as they wait for the machine to reach a verdict.

Even the details in chess fiction mirror chess reality. In Fritz Lieber's 1962 short story "The Moriarty Gambit," Sherlock Holmes faces his archnemesis, Professor Moriarty, in the first round of the London International Chess Tournament of 1883. As play is about to commence, Holmes offers his hand, but Moriarty—in an effort to discombobulate Holmes—does not extend his. In 1978, sixteen years after the story was published, Karpov and Korchnoi first battled it out for the world crown. In the eighth game (the first seven ended in draws) Karpov ignored Korchnoi's outstretched hand; Korchnoi was so rattled that he was promptly trounced.

6-2
DEATH AT THE
CHESSBOARD
White to suffer a stroke in
two, after winning material.

In Agatha Christie's 1927 thriller "A Chess Problem," a chess master succumbs to heart failure in the middle of a tournament game. Six years after Christie penned this story, a man named Dr. Olland suffered a fatal heart attack after his opponent made his twenty-fifth move in an important tournament game. Two moves earlier, Olland's opponent had planted a Bishop on QB6, to reach the position in diagram 6-2. How did Olland win material?

The Queen's Gambit is a major exception to the observation that little that is novel happens in chess fiction. Here a young American woman, Beth Harmon, struggles against formidable obstacles to prove that she is better than the Soviet world champion. Nothing comparable has ever happened in real life. Only a few women in the history of the game have held their own against strong male masters. The reason is not clear. Fischer, who is not known for his tact or eloquence, ascribes the absence of strong female players to the fact that "they're stupid compared to men." Reuben Fine, a psychoanalyst who was at one time the second-ranking chess player in the world, explains in *The Great Chess Movie* that a woman wants a man to take care of her and admire her and that she's not going to win a man over by playing strong chess. Then again, it's hard to imagine how a man might charm the pants off women by his mating attack at the chessboard. Nor is it clear, speaking now sociobiologically instead of psychoanalytically, how chess technique might contribute to a man's genetic investment but not to a woman's.

Fine may sound too analytical, but he wrote the classic work *The Psychology of the Chess Player*. In it he explains how chess "touches upon the conflicts surrounding aggression, homosexuality, masturbation and narcissism." The game, Fine notes, "is more often than not taught to the boy by his father, or a father-substitute, and thus becomes a means of working out the son-father rivalry." Moreover, the King, although the central figure in the game, is impotent compared with the Queen, the mother figure. Fine sees the prohibition against touching the opponent's pieces (except for purposes of capture) and the touch-move rule, according to which if you touch one of your own pieces you are punished by having to move it, as being akin psychodynamically to taboos on homosexuality and masturbation. Inasmuch as the scientific literature contains such provocative insights into the game, is it any wonder that chess has attracted the attention of fiction writers?

Great chess players are like characters in novels, and their lives reek of the make-believe. Could anything be more phantasmagorical than the 1978 Karpov–Korchnoi match, in which

Korchnoi recruited two Indian mystics who were under indict-
ment for murder to meditate in the front row, and Karpov,
who ate quail eggs during the game, asked the parapsychologist Vladimir Zoukhar to sit in the audience and put a hex on
Korchnoi? (Parapsychology proved to be more powerful than
mysticism.) And then there were the well-publicized shenani-
gans of Fischer's match against the Soviet grandmaster Boris
Spassky, whose team ordered the referees to dismantle the
players' chairs in order to make sure that the CIA hadn't
implanted any harmful radiation devices.

Insanity is not a recent development in the chess world. The
great nineteenth-century champion Paul Morphy retreated
into psychosis after a brilliant tournament career that didn't
even last two years. He feared that people were going to destroy his clothes, and he spent much time arranging women's
shoes in a half-circle in his room. The Mexican chess genius
Carlos Torre suffered a psychotic breakdown at the peak of his
career. In 1926 the twenty-two-year-old Torre was playing in a
tournament in New York; while riding on a Fifth Avenue bus,
he suddenly stripped off all his clothes. The Polish master A.
Frydman reportedly parted company with reality in a similar
way, by running nude through a Polish tournament hall,
shouting, "Fire!"

We have looked so far at chess fiction about activity *around*
the chessboard but not *on* it. Of greater interest are literary
works in which the plot unfolds in accordance with the moves
in an actual chess game. The first and most famous example is
Lewis Carroll's *Through the Looking-Glass*, published in 1872.
When Alice steps through the looking-glass, she finds that
she's a White Pawn on a giant chessboard. The frontispiece of
the book shows a chess position with the caption "White Pawn
(Alice) to play and win. . . ." Each move, which corresponds
to an episode in the story, is then listed (diagram 6-3).

The first thing the chess-minded reader notices is that
looking-glass chess bears little resemblance to real chess. White

makes thirteen moves compared with Red's three, and on Red's final move (Q–K1 check), neither side notices that the White King is in check. Moreover, each side misses strong moves. In the diagrammed position, for example, White can force a checkmate in three moves. I leave it to you to show how.

6-3
LOOKING-GLASS CHESS
Alice is the Pawn. White can mate in three, but instead the game drags on with each side passing. The dark pieces represent the red chessmen.

White	Red	White	Red
1. Pass	Q–KR4	8. Q–QB8	Pass
2. P–Q4	Pass	9. P–Q7	N–K2 ch.
3. Q–QB4	Pass	10. N × N	Pass
4. Q–QB5	Pass	11. N–KB5	Pass
5. P–Q5	Pass	12. P–Q8 = Q	Q–K1 ch.
6. Q–KB8	Pass	13. Q–QR6	Pass
7. P–Q6	Pass	14. Q(Alice) × Q mate	

Although the looking-glass game violates both the rules and the logic of chess, it is true to chess in other respects. Alice really has the vision of a Pawn. She sees only what's near her and she talks to a piece only if it's on a square adjacent to her own. Alice has no idea who's running the show, and when she reaches the eighth rank and is crowned Queen, she naively asks if the game is over—ignorant of the fact that the object is checkmate.

All of this becomes clearer if one keeps in mind that *Through the Looking-Glass* is not only a children's fantasy but also a sophisticated commentary on the metaphysical and scientific issues of the day, one of which was the question of free will versus determinism. Carroll's answer, embedded in the metaphor of the chessboard, is that although the world is a deterministic place (the moves Alice and the others make are not of their own choice but are stipulated), the nature of this determinism is not clear (just as the rules and logic of looking-glass chess are not evident).

Although Carroll may have been the first to employ people as chessmen in a work of fiction, the idea itself is not fictitious. In the Middle Ages and the Renaissance the rich and powerful occasionally amused themselves by playing chess with human pieces on huge outdoor boards. An Italian governor in the fifteenth century decided which of two men would marry his daughter by having them play a chess game with live pieces in front of his subjects.

The stakes of a game played with human pieces is carried to a marvelously perverse extreme in Kurt Vonnegut's 1951 story "All the King's Horses," which has been anthologized in *Welcome to the Monkey House*. Colonel Bryan Kelly, his wife, Margaret, their ten-year-old twins, Jerry and Paul, and twelve American enlisted men crash-land in hostile Asian territory ruled by the Communist guerrilla Pi Ying, who exudes the same milk of human kindness as Marlon Brando does in the movie *Apocalypse Now*. Delighted that his captives number sixteen, the Maoist meanie orders them to be the White pieces in a game of chess. If they win, they'll be set free; if they lose, God knows what will happen. But even winning will entail losses. Any human piece that is captured by Pi Ying's enormous inanimate chessmen "will be killed quickly, painlessly, promptly." Colonel Kelly, who commands the White pieces, is the King, his wife is the Queen and his children are the Knights.

As the story unfolds, Vonnegut describes specific moves on the board as the colonel tries to sacrifice the fewest lives in order to win the game and free the rest. Ordinarily a player is not hampered by swapping pieces, but here each exchange brings death. Moreover, Pi Ying moves "with no strategy other than to destroy White men."

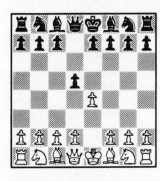

6-4
THE CENTER COUNTER
DEFENSE
A bold bid for early counterplay

Since the plot is so closely connected to the logic of chess, one expects the chess moves to reflect the plot, and the first moves live up to this expectation. Colonel Kelly orders the Pawn in front of him to move forward two squares (in chess notation P–K4, the move with which Fischer opened as White in virtually all his tournament games). The sadistically clever Pi Ying counters with P–Q4, which is known in chess circles as the Center Counter Defense (diagram 6-4). This defense is rarely employed in grandmaster chess because if White now exchanges Pawns, Black's Queen is prematurely brought to the center, where White can harass it. Here, however, the defense is a stroke of genius. White can scarcely trade Pawns because it would mean snuffing out the life of an innocent person. Colonel Kelly is hard pressed to find a better move, however. Advancing the King's Pawn another square, to the fifth rank, would remove the Pawn from the immediate danger, but would expose it to further attack and not contribute to the overall strength of White's position.

Kelly chooses a worse move—and it is at this point that the chess logic of the story collapses. He defends the King's Pawn with the Queen's Pawn, by playing P–Q3 (diagram 6-5). Perhaps he is hoping that Pi Ying will be merciful and not exchange Pawns. The move is actually a horrendous blunder. Pi Ying seizes the chance to take, and kill, the King's Pawn. The colonel responds by taking Pi Ying's Pawn with the Queen's Pawn. And now, if Vonnegut were being true to the sadistic logic he has established, Pi Ying would exchange Queens so that he would have the pleasure of executing Kelly's wife. Not only does Pi Ying forgo QxQ but the possibility is not even mentioned. Instead, Black plays the staid "King's Pawn to King three."

6-5
THE COLONEL BLUNDERS
The exchange of Pawns would expose
Margaret, the colonel's wife, to
execution.

No more moves are given for a while. An hour into the game, we are told that "five Pawns are still alive, among them the young corporal; one Bishop, the nervy pilot; two Rooks; two Knights—ten-year-old frightened Knights; Margaret, a rigid, staring Queen; and himself, the King. The missing four? Butchered—butchered in senseless exchanges that had cost Pi Ying only blocks of wood." Kelly had played with the best interests of his men at heart. He "had moved to defend each of his chessmen at any cost, had risked none in offense. His powerful Queen, Knights, and Rooks stood unused in the relative safety of the two rear rows of squares."

He sees, at this point, that he could checkmate Pi Ying "if only the Black Knight weren't dominating the center of the board." He also comes to the horrible realization that in the present position Pi Ying can finish him off by moving his Queen diagonally to the left three squares in order to put him in check and then delivering mate on the next move.

To distract Pi Ying from this possibility and to dislodge the Black Knight that was obstructing his own winning attack, Kelly decides that he will sacrifice one of his own pieces. "A sacrifice had to be offered Pi Ying's Knight. If Pi Ying accepted the sacriface, the game would be Kelly's. The trap was perfect and deadly save for one detail—bait." With only four seconds left to make a move, he tells Jerry to move forward one square and two to the left. Jerry obliges, trusting his pop. Pi Ying is delightfully baffled by this offer of the colonel's child. The colonel buries his head in his hands, pretending to have blundered. Pi Ying orders his Knight to move to King Bishop's six, capturing Jerry.

The game is now the colonel's. He tells his wife to capture a Black Pawn, putting the King in check. The King retreats one square to its left. At this point the colonel checks again by instructing the Bishop to "Move diagonally one square toward me." Black gets out of check by interposing his Queen between his King and the offending Bishop. Now, White's farthest-advanced Pawn takes the Queen and Black is checkmated.

I have a whopper of a brain buster for you. Is there any chess truth to the moves described in the last four paragraphs? In other words, can you set up a chess position in accordance with what Vonnegut tells us about the position "an hour into the game"? The position must lead to checkmate if one follows the moves that Vonnegut describes. Perhaps there's no such position. After all, we have already seen one major instance in which Vonnegut betrays chess logic by not playing an obvious move that the logic of his story demands. Let me warn you that I spent much time on this problem before reaching a decision.

Poul Anderson's 1954 story "The Immortal Game" is faith-

ful both to the rules and to the logic of chess because it is
chiefly told from the point of view of an animated medieval
chess piece, Rogard the Bishop, who is eager to help his side,
the kingdom of Cinnabar, defeat the enemy, the kingdom of
Leukas. The story is a complex fantasy that involves a host of
characters (Sir Ocher, Rogard, Flambard, Evyan the Fair,
Carlon, Columbard, Earl Ferric, Sir Cupran, Mikillati, Dol-
ora, Sorkas, Earl Rafaeon, Sir Theutas, Ulfar, Earl Aracle and
so on) whose movements the reader must painstakingly track
if he is to play out the story on a chessboard. Vigilance will
enable the reader to make chess sense out of such statements

6-6
THE IMMORTAL GAME
OF 1851
Anderssen v. Kieseritzky
White offers the immortal
sacrifice of both Rooks.

6-7
THE IMMORTAL MATE
Anderssen v. Kieseritzky
White to mate in three.

as "The Leukan Bishop was poised to rush in with his great
mace should Flambard, for safety, seek to change with Earl
Ferric as the Law permitted."

Near the end of the story, the point of view abruptly
changes to that of a scientist and a visiting colleague who are
watching the chess game: "I see." The visitor nodded. "Individual computers, each controlling their own robot piece by a
light beam, and all the computers on a given side linked to
form a sort of group-mind constrained to obey the rules of

chess and make the best possible moves. Very nice. And it's a pretty cute notion of yours, making the robots look like medieval armies."

The visitor then points out, to the surprise of the scientist, that the computers are re-creating a classic game, known in chess circles as the "the Immortal Game," played between Adolf Anderssen and L. Kieseritzky in a famous London tournament in 1851. On the eighteenth move, Anderssen offered the "immortal" sacrifice of both Rooks, by shifting the Bishop from B4 to Q6 (diagram 6-6). In the story, the immortal sacrifice is described this way: "Rogard cast a fleeting glance at Bishop Sorkas. The lean white-caped form was gliding forth, mace swinging loose in one hand, and there was a little sleepy smile on the pale face. No dismay—? Sorkas halted, facing Rogard, and smiled a little wider, skinning his teeth without humor. 'You can kill me if you wish,' he said softly. 'But do you?' " Sorkas's smile can only mean that something horrible is in store for Cinnabar should Rogard capture him. What is it?

Three moves later, after Kieseritzky captured both White Rooks, Anderssen unveiled a three-move mating combination (diagram 6-7). Can you find it?

At this point in the story, the visitor suggests that the computers might have consciousness because the robot pieces are enthusiastically "jumping inside their squares, waving their arms, batting at each other with their weapons." The scientist dismisses this out of hand, but the visitor is unrelenting. "How do you know," he asks, "that they don't receive the data of the moves as their own equivalent of blood, sweat and tears?" The scientist simply grunts and turns off the computers as White checkmates Black.

The second move in the Immortal Game (P–KB4) initiates an opening called the King's Gambit, in which White gives up a Pawn in return for greater control of the center of the board. The danger of the opening is that the White King is exposed along the K1–KR4 diagonal. In an anonymous poem, pub-

lished in the *St. Louis Globe-Democrat,* a woodpusher behind
the White pieces contributes to this danger, in the interest of
discombobulating his opponent, by moving his King out along
the exposed diagonal. Set up your pieces and follow along:

> In Seattle, last summer, with nothing to do,
> I went to the chess club and there met a Jew
> From New Orleans, a rabbi—no matter what name—
> Perhaps you have met him, or heard of the same;
> He's a player of note, and his problems in chess
> Get some mighty good players in an awful bad mess.
> He asked, "Do you play, sir?" I said: "Just a little."
> "Well, sit you down here, and let's have a skittle."
> He glanced round the room: "I judge by the looks
> That you players here are not up in the books."
> I replied with a laugh, and a gentle a-hem,
> "No, we long, long ago got far beyond them."
> With a shrug of his shoulders, the Whites he gave me.
> "Make your opening," he said, "and we will soon see."
> I played P to K's fourth, which he seemed to approve,
> And replied with the same; 'twas a very good move.
> The King's Bishop's Pawn I put out with some force,
> And he took it at once, as a matter of course.
> But judge the expression that came over his face
> When I played out my King to K.B.'s second place.
> "Oh, well," said the rabbi, "that looks a bit hazy,
> If I'm any judge, the King's Gambit gone crazy."
> So he out with his Queen and he checked at R's five.
> With the evident purpose to flay me alive.
> With a soft, gentle push I interposed Pawn,
> He took it with his, in a moment 'twas gone.
> He thundered out "check" in such stentorian tones,
> That it gave me the shivers, a quake in the bones;
> But I slipped the King over N's 2d square,
> Then he took my Rook's Pawn with his, and said, "There,
> You must take that with your Rook, and then it is plain

That my Queen takes the other one out in the main;
And with no Pawns on King's side, I must say I can't see
How you can prevent my Queening my three—
Should the game ever get to the point where they're needed."
"I don't think it will," I replied. But he heeded
Me not; and when he captured my little King's P
I brought my Knight to the King's Bishop's three;
Next came Pawn to Queen's four, to free up his house,
I replied with my Queen's Knight, attacking his spouse,
Which he played to N's third, giving check to my King,
At the same time remarking, "I'm on to this thing."

6-8
THE KING'S OWN OPENING
White to win the Black Queen.

The King to Rook's square I quietly played,
And QB to N's fifth he likewise essayed.
Not wishing that harm should come to my "hoss,"
I transferred King's Rook, from his second, across
To N's 2. He now thought to win at a canter.
So he took up his Queen, and at Rook's 4, instanter,
He put her and checked; but I moved to N's square,
And he, little dreaming of the trap that was there,
Whipped off my poor Knight, as he laughingly said,
"That horse is of no use, so off comes his head."
My Knight, he is gone— Oh, alas, 'tis too true,
But I'll interpose Bishop, and I'll see what he'll do.
"Well, if you want me to take all your pieces and done,

Shove 'em out and I'll capture them, every darn one."
So he grabbed the poor prelate at once by the neck,
And I somewhat surprised him with RxB, check.
Not till then did the truth dawn clear on his brain,
And he tried hard to save his fair Queen, but in vain.
"Now what kind of game do you say you call that?"
"The KING'S OWN," I replied, "and I'll bet you a hat
You can't find it in any or all the chess books
You have studied," and I judged from his looks
That he somewhat doubted when I told him the same
Was a notion of Pollack's, who gave it that name.

There actually was a Pollack, the champion of Ireland in the
early 1890s, who apparently played this ridiculous opening.

Fiction that does justice to the moves of chess tends to be
much less ambitious than Carroll's or Vonnegut's work, in
which the main action takes place on a chessboard. But stories
about chess and its devotees sometimes include interesting positions. In Kester Svendsen's 1947 story "Last Round," an
aging master who has not won a tournament in ten years sets
out to play the perfect game against the Soviet champion
Rolavsky. As White in the position in diagram 6-9, the old
master unleashes a startling winning combination. Can you
find it?

6-9
THE PERFECT GAME
Old Master v. Soviet Champion
White to win.

In the game between Holmes (White) and Moriarty (Black) in "The Moriarty Gambit," the position in diagram 6-10 is reached after the nineteenth move. When he replays the game for Watson, Holmes says at this point, "I surveyed the board and said quietly, 'It is mate in five moves, Professor Moriarty.' And then I did a rather extraordinary thing, Watson—I reached across the table and for a moment lightly laid my right hand on his left shoulder. He drew back with a snarl." Can you find the mate?

6-10
THE EPAULETTE MATE
Sherlock Holmes v. Moriarty
White to mate in five.

6-11
ALIBI FOR A THEFT
Sir James Winslade v. Lord Churt

Raymond Allen, in his 1916 tale "A Happy Solution," brilliantly works a chess puzzle into a crime story. A £1,000 note, earmarked for the Red Cross, is stolen while Sir James Winslade is playing chess with Lord Churt at the odds of the Queen's Rook. Winslade and Churt do not distinctly remember that Gornay, the secretary, was present during their game, but the comments he made in the postmortem analysis of the game, when the final position was set up on the board (diagram 6-11), indicates that he knew about the previous play and, hence, was there when the game was played. Gornay's postgame comment is that Black might have been better off taking the Queen with the Bishop's Pawn instead of with the

Rook's Pawn. Gornay's alibi is smashed when someone points out that he could have known from the final position that the Black Pawn on QN3 took a Queen. How could he have known this?

Another twist in the story is that Black, who was on the move in the final position, resigned in the face of the mating attack Q–R6–N7 or N–N4–R6. But it is Black who can win in the diagrammed position, as Gornay pointed out. What line of play did he have in mind?

ANSWERS

The key move in Nabokov's mate-in-three puzzle is Q–R7. Then 1...K–N1 2. RxP! (not 2. R–Q1, which is defeated by 2...K–B1) K–B1 3. R–R8 mate or 1...P–R7 2. Q–N1! (not 2. R–Q1, which is defeated by P=Q pinning the Rook) K–R2 3. RxP mate. In Nabokov's retract-a-move problem White's last move was capturing a Black Knight on QB8 with a Pawn on Q7, which is promoted to a Rook. Instead, White should use the Pawn to capture the Black Rook, making the Pawn a Knight.

Two moves before Olland had a heart attack, he played his Knight to Q6, forking Black's Queen and Rook. Black moved his Queen to B2. White grabbed the Rook with his Knight and Black took back with his Bishop. Then White keeled over.

In the looking-glass game, White can deliver mate without Alice's assistance, by first checking with the Knight on N3. If the Red King retreats to Q5 or Q6, White mates by playing his Queen to QB3. The Red King could have postponed the agony a move by retreating instead to K4. In that case, the White Queen checks on QB5, driving the King to K3, and mates on Q6.

. . .

After much effort, I was able to construct a position—I should say two positions—corresponding to the chess information Vonnegut provides (diagrams 6-12 and 6-13). The two positions come from an ambiguity in the story. When Vonnegut writes that Pi Ying is threatening a two-move checkmate by moving his Queen diagonally three squares to the left, does he mean Pi Ying's left or the colonel's left? The more natural interpretation is Pi Ying's left, but I have constructed a position for each possibility. In diagram 6-12 the threatened mate

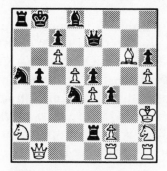

6-12
KURT VONNEGUT'S
DEATH GAME
Captive American v.
Sadistic Captor

6-13
ALTERNATIVE DEATH

is Q–R5 check followed by Q–N6 (the Queen is immune to capture because the Rook pins the Pawn). By guarding the Black Pawn on N4 and by covering the KB4 square, the central Black Knight stops a mating attack by Kelly. Kelly tries to divert the Knight by moving Jerry, a white Knight, to KB3. Eager for blood, Pi Ying falls for NxN. Kelly responds with QxP check and Black retreats his King to QB1. (If Black played instead K–R2, mate follows after QxN check, Q–N5 check and Q–N7 mate.) White plays B–B5 check and Black interposes his Queen on Q2. White then mates with PxQ, and Kelly's men have won their freedom.

In diagram 6-13 Kelly's mate is the same, but Pi Ying's threat begins with a Queen move in the opposite direction. If it were Pi Ying's move, he could mate by Q–N5 check and N–N2 discovered mate.

Although all this squares with what Vonnegut says about chess moves, it is probably just a fluke. It would have taken many moves and much absurd maneuvering to reach either of the diagrammed positions. There would have been no time for that because Pi Ying, savoring each execution, would have forced the exchange of many more pieces.

In the Immortal Game the White Bishop is immune to capture because of 19. NxB check K–Q1 (or 19 . . . K–B1 20. QxP mate) 20. NxP check K–K1 21. N–Q6 check K–K1 22. Q–B8 mate. The three-move combination at the end of the game involves a Queen sacrifice to divert the Knight from its coverage of K2: 21. NxP check K–Q1 22. Q–B6 check NxQ 23. B–K7 mate. Note that Black is mated in spite of his being in possession of *all* of his forces (excluding Pawns).

The old master mates the Soviet champion: 1. Q–K8 check RxQ 2. PxR (becoming a Queen and delivering check) BxQ 3. BxQP mate. Joel Craft informed me that the game in this story is not fictitious; it was played in 1883 between Charousek and Wallner in Kassa, Hungary. This supports my observation that there is little fiction in chess fiction. Nor is the "perfect game" in this story all that perfect. As Blaine Wickens pointed out, another mate is also possible and perhaps more spectacular: 1. BxP check B(or P)xB 2. Q–K8 check BxQ 3. PxB, becoming a Queen and delivering mate.

Holmes mates Moriarty: 1. QxP check K–Q1 2. Q–B8 check K–K2 3. B–N4 check K–B3 4. Q–B5 check K–N2 5. QxNP mate. With customary wryness, Holmes tells Watson, "And now in the moment of my triumph, the meaning of my shoulder-touch must have become clear to Moriarty. It was an epaulette mate—the Black Pawns standing to either side of his King, like epaulettes on the shoulders of Black royalty, prevented him from moving aside from my Queen's fatal check. In retrospect I like to think that my shoulder-touch also foreshadowed the day when I hauled off the Napoleon of British crime to British justice."

The clever Gornay could have discerned the fate of the White Queen from the final position. Remember that White began without his Queen's Rook, and judging from the final position, it is clear that the King's Rook was captured on KR1, KN1 or KR2 because it was hemmed into that corner of the board. Only two Black pieces were captured in the course of the game, and they had to be captured by the White Pawns that ended up on K5 and B3 because that is the only way there could be two White Pawns on both the King's file and the Queen's Bishop's file. What happened to the White Queen's Rook's Pawn? Since it didn't capture anything (all captures are accounted for), it had to have traveled all the way to the eighth rank and been promoted to a piece. The promotion occurred after the Black Pawn capture on QN3; otherwise, the White Pawn could not have snuck by. Whatever White piece was captured on QN3 (and it could not have been a Rook because their absence from the board has already been explained) was regenerated when the White Pawn reached QR8. But which piece was regenerated? If it had been a Knight or a Bishop, it would now be standing on the QR8 square or have been captured—neither of which is the case. Therefore, it is the sole remaining piece: the Queen. Consequently, Gornay could have determined—not from watching the game but from analyzing the final position—that Black had captured a Queen on QN3.
Gornay also realized that Black could win the game in the final position by playing 1 . . . P–K6 to hem in the White King. If White proceeds with his attack by 2. Q–R6, then

Black sacrifices his Queen with 2 . . . Q–R5 check. No matter whether the White Queen or Bishop takes the Black Queen, the game would proceed 3 . . . B–B5 4. N–N3 BxN with mate to follow after the Black Rook goes to R8. If White attacks instead with 2. N–N4, Black plays QxN. Then 3. Q(orP)xQ B–B5 as before or 3. Q–R6 Q–R5 check as before. If White chooses not to attack but to play 2. P–KN4, Black plays 2 . . . B–N6 3. NxB QxN and wins after the Rook reaches the eighth rank.

I want to acknowledge my debt to Bruce Pandolfini, the chess columnist of the *Litchfield County* (Connecticut) *Times*, who called my attention to many chess problems in literature.

7
Timid Virgins Make Dull Company: A Trip Down Memory Lane

Thirty days hath September
All the rest I can't remember.
—Anonymous

To better herself, Lora was taking courses at night school toward a doctorate in comparative extraterrestrial anatomy. For the past week and a half she had been studying for her finals, much to the neglect of me and my work at the Institute. As a result, I was somewhat down in the mouth.

I had been sitting next to her, watching her study for what seemed like eternity, when she finally spoke: "I'll never master this material, Crypy. There's too much to learn. How am I supposed to remember that Earthlings have two hundred and six bones, whereas Venusians have two hundred and eight? And then, on top of the biology, there's a lot of astrophysics I need to know. How can I be expected to memorize the way stars are classified on the basis of temperature?"

I was not impressed. "Oh, be a fine girl," I told her. "Kiss me right now, sweetheart."

"You're so very helpful," she replied. "I have tons of work to do. What's really bad is that I can't even read my own notes. I'm going to have to call up Tillie in order to find out the names of the wristbones."

I laughed. "Just remember," I said, "never lower Tillie's pants. Mamma might come home."

"You silly goose. I'm actually feeling better. I think I'll ace my courses—thanks to you."

Now tell me, what was going on in our conversation? Was I deranged and Lora sarcastic? Please read no further until you've decided.

Our conversation, believe it or not, was a wonderful example of what modern psychologists call total verbal communication. My first statement ("Oh, be a fine girl. Kiss me right now, sweetheart") is a mnemonic, or memory aid, for keeping track of how stars are classified on the basis of temperature. There are ten stellar classes, each designated by a letter; they are, from hottest to coldest, O, B, A, F, G, K, M, R, N and S. The initial letters of the words in the mnemonic correspond to the stellar designations. The mnemonic was invented by George Gamow, the celebrated astrophysicist and popularizer of science.

My second statement ("Never lower Tillie's pants. Mamma might come home") is a mnemonic for the eight wristbones: navicular, lunate, triangular, pisiform, multangular greater, multangular lesser, capitate and hamate. Here the initial letters in the mnemonic correspond to the initial letters of the bones.

Mnemosyne was the Greek goddess of memory, and mnemonics were widely used in ancient Greece and Rome in the study of history and formal logic. Today, virtually everyone makes use of mnemonics, whether or not one knows the word or how to pronounce it. All Americans rely on the verse: "Thirty days hath September, April, June and November. When short February's done, all the rest have thirty-one."

A mnemonic is successful if it can be committed to memory more easily than that for which it stands. The more offbeat it is, the easier it is to remember. Consequently, many mnemonics are risqué, even scatological. Every medical student knows a host of X-rated mnemonics for remembering the names of bones and other parts of the body.

Many common mnemonics involve the spelling of words. "*I* before *e* except after *c* or when rhyming with *a* as in *neighbor* and *weigh*" reassures us that *friend*, say, is spelled correctly. "The principal is your pal" succinctly captures the fact that the kind of principal who runs a school is spelled with *pal* at the end. The first letters of "George Eaton's old granny rode a pig home yesterday" spell *geography*, although it is not clear to me why such a mnemonic is necessary.

Some mnemonics are not common, but should be. More people would be on time if they kept in mind the phrase "Spring forward, fall backward," which indicates the direction to adjust the clock at the beginning and end of daylight saving time.

Certain memory aids depend on the length of words. One can remember how to distinguish the port side of a ship from the starboard because the shorter words *port* and *left* correspond, as do the longer words *starboard* and *right*.

Mnemonics have also been created for provincial things. "Old maids never wed and have babies" expresses where the train stops on the main line out of Philadelphia. The first letters of the words in the mnemonic correspond respectively to the first letters of the train stops: Overbrook, Merion, Narberth, Wynnewood, Ardmore, Haverford and Bryn Mawr.

The correspondence of initial letters is the key to many mnemonics. The initial letters in the following sentences are the initial letters of the presidents in order: "Washington and Jefferson made many a joke. Van Buren had to put the frying pan back. Lincoln just gasped, 'Heaven guard America.' Cleveland had coats made ready to wear home. Coolidge hur-

ried right to every kitchen jar nook. Ford capitulated readily."
(I will spare you a list of the presidents.)

History is also captured by a catchy mnemonic verse that
recounts the fate of the six wives of Henry VIII:

Divorced, beheaded, died.
Divorced, beheaded, survived.

Mathematics has also fathered numerous mnemonics. Sir
James Jeans, an early pioneer of quantum physics, once de-
clared, "How I want a drink—alcoholic, of course—after the
heavy chapters involving quantum mechanics." Jeans was not
confiding that he was a lush but providing a useful mnemonic
for the expansion of π to fifteen places. The number of letters
in each word in the mnemonic provides one digit in the expansion. Jean's sobering statement yields the following for π:
3.14159265358979.

The familiar constant π is equal to the circumference of any
circle divided by its diameter. Although the constant was not
designated by the symbol π until the eighteenth century, the
Egyptians and Babylonians understood the concept as early as
2000 B.C. The Babylonians thought π was equal to 3⅛. Now,
with the aid of the computer, mathematicians have been able
to expand π with mind-boggling precision. In 1967 a computer in Paris spent forty-four hours and forty-five minutes
determining the expansion to 500,000 decimal places. In 1982
a Japanese supercomputer extended the expansion to a whop-
ping 4 million digits.

It may come as a surprise that the constant π is fundamental
to much more than circles. In fact, it comes up frequently in
all areas of mathematics. In 1777, the French naturalist Comte
de Buffon discovered that π has a peculiar role in probability.
He was interested in the probability of randomly dropping a
needle of length L onto a series of parallel lines a distance D
apart, where D exceeds L (see diagram 7-1). What, Buffon
wondered, was the probability of the needle's landing on one

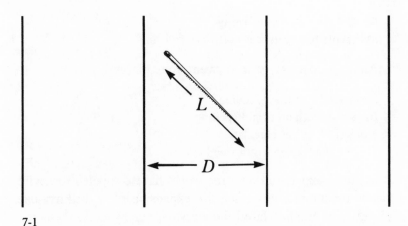

7-1

of the lines? He computed it to be equal to $2L/\pi D$, or twice the needle's length divided by π times the line spacing. The equation suggests a novel way of computing π: Measure the probability empirically by dropping the needle thousands of times on the lines. Multiply this probability by D and divide by $2L$. During the Civil War, a Captain Fox did just that while nursing his war wounds. In 1901, the Italian mathematician Lazzarini dropped a needle 3,400 times and obtained a value for π of 3.14.

Poor π has been subjected to more mnemonic abuse than anything else our species has ever tried to remember. For five places there's the simple "Yes, I know a digit." For eight places, who could forget the question "May I have a large container of coffee"? The lament "How I wish I could recollect pi easily today" gives π to nine places. The 1926 *Chambers's Encyclopaedia* includes a mnemonic for eleven places: "But I must a while endeavour to reckon right the ratio." The success of this mnemonic, however, depends on your remembering to spell *endeavor* the British way, which is bloody unlikely.

Most of the longer mnemonics for π are in verse. For thirteen places there's:

See, I have a rhyme assisting
My feeble brain, its tasks ofttimes resisting.

Another poem gives π to twenty-one places:

Sir, I send a rhyme excelling
In sacred truth and rigid spelling.
Numerical sprites elucidate.
For me the lexicon's dull weight.

Memory experts all over the world have competed to devise clever mnemonic verses for the expansion of π to thirty-one places. The English fared the worst:

Now I know a spell unfailing
An artful charm for tasks awailing
Intricate results entailing
Not in too exacting mood
(Poetry is pretty good.)
Try the talisman.
Let be adverse ingenuity.

I daresay that it may be easier to remember 3.1415926535897932384626433383279 than it is to commit to memory the above "poem."

In any event, French mnemonicists came up with a bombastic verse that also yields π to thirty-one places.

Que j'aime à faire apprendre un nombre utile aux sages!
Immortel Archimède, sublime ingénieur
Qui de ton jugement peut sonder la valeur?
Pour moi ton problème eut de pareils avantages?

The verse can be translated "How I want to teach a useful number to wise men! Immortal Archimedes, sublime engineer, who can plumb the value of your judgment? For me your problem had similar advantages." The mnemonic is quite appropriate because Archimedes made an early contribution to the theory of π: in the third century B.C. he proved that π has a value of between $3\frac{1}{7}$ and $3\frac{10}{71}$.

To regain England's lead in mnemonic high jinks, Lord Balfour of Burleigh held a mnemonic competition in 1951 in *The Dark Horse*, the house organ of Lloyds Bank International. Balfour's bid to outdo the French turned out to be pie in the sky. The winning submission provided π to the same thirty-one places that the French verse did:

Now I will a rhyme construct,
By chosen words the young instruct,
Cunningly devised endeavour.
Con it and remember ever.
Widths in circle here you see
Sketched out in strange obscurity.

MNEMONIC QUIZ

I have collected twenty-six mnemonics. Following the mnemonics is a list of what they stand for, but the items on the list are not in order. The puzzle is to find what each mnemonic represents.

1. Kangaroos respond when lemmings run counterclockwise.
2. Tully Zucker's bowels move constantly.
3. Homes.
4. My very educated mother just served us nine pickles.
5. By omnibus I traveled to Brooklyn.
6. Big chief Sohcahtoa.
7. Camels often sit down carefully. Perhaps their joints creak. Possibly, early oiling might prevent painful rheumatism.
8. Working wives have seldom had really jazzy hemlines. Triple-E rubbers hardly help. Hairstyles everywhere even resemble haystacks, higher every month, enormous! Jolly courtiers clothe jades, whose men are grateful for what virility endures; gaudy, effete gentlemen expire, cheering.

9. Bourgeois dreamy damsel goads horny short sidekicks.
10. Every good boy deserves fudge.
11. Retaliating for long frustration, Moses badgered hostile leader, demanding freedom.
12. On old Olympus' towering top, a fat-assed German vends snowy hops.
13. Do men ever visit Boston?
14. Poor Queen Victoria eats crow at Christmas.
15. Soon super soporific stupor spreads.
16. D. C. Van Dissel.
17. A boy now will mention all the horrid battles till Bosworth.
18. Bless my dear Aunt Sally.
19. Every mother beams at reared rascals achieving scholarly success.
20. Timid virgins make dull company.
21. King Philip came over from glorious Scotland.
22. The girls could flirt and other queer things could do.
23. Now I live a drear existence in ragged suits and cruel taxation suffering.
24. Triple D and B.
25. See the dog jump in a circle. Leave her home to entertain editors.
26. Bad boys rape our young girls, but Violet gives willingly.

WHAT THEY MEAN

A. Absolute zero.
B. The Linnaean system of classification.
C. Battles of the Wars of the Roses.
D. The cranial nerves.
E. English monarchs.
F. The calculations a navigator must perform in order to determine position.
G. The expansion of π.
H. The spelling of *embarrass*.
 I. The hills of Rome.
J. The weapons in the board game Clue.
K. The Great Lakes.

L. The notes on a musical scale.
M. The expansion of the transcendental number *e*.
N. The plagues of Egypt.
O. The geological divisions.
P. The order in which algebraic operations should be performed.
Q. The planets.
R. The hierarchy of the English peerage.
S. The trigonometric functions.
T. The Mohs' scale of mineral hardness.
U. Snow White's woodland companions.
V. What a physician is supposed to pay attention to when he admits a patient to a hospital.
W. The branches of the facial nerve.
X. The color coding on electrical resistors.
Y. The departments in the federal government in the order in which they were created.
Z. The names of the least conservative aides in the Reagan White House.

ANSWERS

1J. The weapons in Clue: knife, revolver, wrench, lead pipe, rope, candlestick.

2W. The branches of the facial nerve: temporal, zygomatic, buccal, mewtal, cervical.

3K. The Great Lakes: Huron, Ontario, Michigan, Erie, Superior.

4Q. The nine planets in order of their distance from the sun: Mercury, Venus, Earth, Mars, Jupiter, Saturn, Uranus, Neptune, Pluto. Other versions of the mnemonic substitute *earnest* for *educated* and *pizzas* for *pickles*.

5M. The transcendental number *e*: 2.71828. Two additional digits are provided by the sentence "It enables a numskull to memorize a quantity." A French mnemonic gives eleven digits: *"Tu aideras à rappeler ta quantité à beaucoup de docteurs amis"* ("You will help many friendly scholars to recall your quantity").

6S. *Sohcahtoa* is an acronym for "**S**ine **O**pposite **H**ypotenuse,

Cosine Adjacent Hypotenuse, Tangent Opposite Adjacent," which is a shorthand way of keeping track of the trigonometric functions. The schoolmarm who taught me trig told me I could remember *Sohcahtoa* if I pronounced it as if it were the name of an Indian chief. But how does one avoid confusing big chief Sohcahtoa with big chief Sahcohtoa?

A less confusing mnemonic is the sentence "Some of her children are having trouble over algebra." Nevertheless, the sentence is quite dull and thus easily forgettable. To help future generations master trigonometry, Michael Steuben held a mnemonic competition in *Capital M*, the newsletter of the Washington, D.C., chapter of MENSA. My favorite entries are "Sex on holidays can activate happy times over all" and "Showing one's hand can affect how the opposition advances." In each case, the first letters can be combined to spell *Sohcahtoa*.

7O. The geological divisions: Cambrian, Ordovician, Silurian, Devonian, Carboniferous, Permian, Triassic, Jurassic, Cretaceous, Paleocene, Eocene, Oligocene, Miocene, Pliocene, Pleistocene, Recent.

8E. All the English monarchs from William the Conqueror to the current Prince of Wales: William I, William II, Henry I, Stephen, Henry II, Richard I, John, Henry III, Edward I, Edward II, Edward III, Richard II, Henry IV, Henry V, Henry VI, Edward IV, Edward V, Richard III, Henry VII, Henry VIII, Edward VI, Mary I, Elizabeth I, James I, Charles I, Charles II, James II, William and Mary, Anne, George I, George II, George III, George IV, William IV, Victoria, Edward VII, George V, Edward VIII, George VI, Elizabeth II, Charles III. In the mnemonic, *Triple-E* stands for Edward I, II and III, and *grateful for* represents the first four Georges. The mnemonic errs in not mentioning William III as reigning apart from Mary.

Another mnemonic gives the monarchs from William the Conqueror to George VI, but leaves out John, of Magna Carta fame:

Willie, Willie, Harry, Stee.
Harry, Dick, Harry Three.

One, Two, Three Neds, Richard Two.
Harry Four, Five, Six. Then who?
Edward Four, Five, Dick the Bad.
Harrys twain and Ned the Lad.
Mary, Bessie, James the Vain.
Charles, Charles, James again.
William and Mary, Anna Gloria.
Four Georges, William and Victoria.
Edward the Seventh next, and then
George the Fifth in 1910.
Edward the Eighth soon abdicated.
And so a George was reinstated.

9U. Snow White's seven dwarfs: Bashful, Doc, Dopey, Grumpy, Happy, Sleepy, Sneezy.

10L. The notes of a musical scale: E, G, B, D, F.

11N. The plagues of Egypt: river turned to blood, frogs, lice, flies, murrain, boils, hail, locusts, darkness, firstborn slain. In *The Passover Haggadah* a mnemonic provides the first letters of the Hebrew words for the ten plagues. At the seder it is the custom to sprinkle wine at the mention of each word in the mnemonic.

12D. The twelve cranial nerves: olfactory, optic, oculomotor, trochlear, trigeminal, abducens, facial, acoustic, glossopharyngeal, vagus, spinal accessory, hypoglossal.

13R. The hierarchy of the English peerage: duke, marquess, earl, viscount, baron.

14I. The seven hills of Rome: Palatine, Quirinal, Viminal, Esquiline, Capitoline, Aventine, Caelian.

15A. Absolute zero: −459.67°F.

16V. What a physician is supposed to pay attention to when admitting a patient to the hospital: diagnosis, condition, vital signs, ambulation, nursing orders, diet, intake and output, symptomatic drugs, specific drugs, examinations, laboratory.

17C. Battles of the Wars of the Roses: St. Albans, Blore Heath, Northampton, Wakefield, Mortimer's Cross, second St. Albans, Towton, Hedgeley Moor, Barnet, Tewkesbury, Bosworth Field.

18P. The order in which algebraic operations should be performed: brackets, multiplication, division, addition, subtraction.

19H. The spelling of *embarrass*.

20F. Interpreted backward, this mnemonic tells a navigator the order in which to do calculations: compass, deviation, magnetic, variation, true.

21B. The Linnaean system of classification: kingdom, phylum, class, order, family, genus, species.

22T. The Mohs' scale of mineral hardness (from softest to hardest): talc, gypsum, calcite, fluorite, apatite, orthoclase, quartz, topaz, corundum, diamond.

23G. π to thirteen places: 3.141592653589.

24Z. On April 30, 1983, *The New York Times* reported that on a recent trip on the White House staff and press plane, an announcement was made about the "triple D and B combination," a reference to Reagan's three moderate aides whose last names start with *D* (Michael Deaver, Richard Darman and Kenneth Duberstein) and the one moderate aide whose last initial is *B* (James Baker).

25Y. The departments in the federal government in order of their creation: State, Treasury, Defense, Justice, Interior, Agriculture, Commerce, Labor, Health, Housing, Transportation, Energy, Education.

26X. The color coding on electrical resistors: black, brown, red, orange, yellow, green, blue, violet, gray, white. Each color corresponds to a digit from 0 to 9. In spite of its racy tone, this mnemonic is one of the most popular; it was taught to me in the third grade.

I challenge you to devise mnemonics for such things as the ten events in the Olympic decathlon, the names of the vice-presidents of the United States in chronological order, the twelve Apostles of Jesus, the Watergate Seven, the Nine Muses and the Seven Deadly Sins.

8
Get Off the Earth and Other Puzzles from Brooklyn

The obvious way to profit from a puzzle column is to win the contests that appear in it, but leave it to readers to find more ingenious ones. On March 2, 1963, *The Harvard Crimson* ran a short piece on the front page headlined LOCAL MERCHANTS TAKE 5 COUNTERFEIT $20 BILLS. The story said: "Five counterfeit $20 bills, made by taping together pieces of cut-up $10's and $20's, have been received by Harvard Square merchants, Cambridge police announced Tuesday. . . . The 'remodeled' currency is made about one-quarter inch shorter than normal bills, [Lt. Det. Alfred E.] Marckini said, so that the counterfeiters can make 12 bills out of 10." A similar incident occurred in Idaho and was covered by the *Des Moines Register*, writes Martin Gardner in his numerological fantasy *The Incredible Dr. Matrix*.

The counterfeiting was inspired by Gardner's puzzle column in the January 1963 issue of *Scientific American*. Gardner described a method for cutting up fourteen bills and rearranging the pieces to make fifteen, each bill one-fifteenth shorter than the normal piece of currency. The method, which can be applied to things other than money, was championed at the turn of the century by the greatest paradoxologist this country has ever known, a Brooklynite named Sam Loyd.

Who is this Loyd fellow, you may wonder, whom I have often praised in glowing terms that are not usually part of my decidedly curmudgeonish vocabulary? Perhaps the best introduction to him can be made in his own words, quoted in 1911 in the classy women's monthly *Delineator:* "I was born in Philadelphia in 1841. One of my ancestors was a Colonial governor of Pennsylvania, and my mother was a Singer, so that I am a cousin of John Singer Sargent, the portrait-painter. You ask me to what I attribute my propensity for puzzles, and I can only answer, the Lord."

The youngest of eight children, Loyd exhibited an interest in chess, music, art, magic and ventriloquism. As a wee tot, he drove a servant to resign by making the woman hear "voices" coming from the chimney.

His passion for fooling people did not abate with age. Alain White's 1913 work, *Sam Loyd and His Chess Problems,* which is still available, states that in adulthood Loyd once took his family on a steamboat cruise. A wicked storm drove all the passengers from the sun deck into the cabin, but Loyd found a pack of cards and saved the day by putting on a magic show. His last trick was an experiment in thought transmission. A volunteer was asked to blindfold Loyd's fifteen-year-old son, Sammy, who was sitting with his back turned at the other end of the cabin. Loyd then picked a card at random from the deck and held it up, with the back of the card toward the boy. "What card is this?" Loyd asked. The boy immediately gave the correct answer. Again and again Loyd did the trick, repeatedly stumping everyone on board.

Sometime later he revealed the hocus-pocus: "Of course Sammy does not know what card I draw out, but simply moves his lips in reply to my questions, while I supply his voice by ventriloquism." On another occasion when Loyd performed the trick, White wrote, "he pretended that the boy couldn't always tell the right card—he would then try several times until, by an apparently great strain, the answer was forthcoming. After the performance a benevolent old gentleman came up to him and urged him to give up doing this mental telepathy, as it was too great a strain on the boy and must sooner or later result injuriously!"

Loyd was an incorrigible prankster, particularly when miffed. In 1907, when he was sixty-six, he was interviewed by Walter Prichard Eaton for the London monthly *Strand*. At one point Eaton showed little interest in a puzzle Loyd was describing. As Eaton put it:

Mr. Loyd looked grieved at the interviewer's rude show of indifference, much as an artist looks when you ignore his pictures. Then his face lit up with an evil light, masked behind a bland smile. "Did you ever see the puzzle I made for John A. McCall, when he was president of the New York Life [Insurance Company]?" he asked.

I was forced to admit that I hadn't. From a mysterious corner of his desk he drew forth a small stick, some six inches long, cut to represent a toy policeman's billy. It was hung on a green string loop, the loop being almost but not quite as long as the stick. Holding this curious toy in his hand, Mr. Loyd said, "Once John A. McCall sent for me and suggested that I invent something in the puzzle line for his [insurance] agents to use that would pleasantly keep their mission in folks' mind. The next day I returned with this. He said 'H'm,' dangling it on his finger, 'very neat, but hardly striking, I should say. How do you propose to use it?' I grasped the lapel of his coat so," and Sam Loyd seized mine. "I slipped the string through the buttonhole so," and he slipped the string through my buttonhole; "and then I pushed the stick so," and he did something with the stick so quickly that I couldn't follow; "and then I said, 'Mr. McCall, I'll bet you a hundred dollars to one that you can't get that off in half an hour, without cutting the string.' "

A horrible fear smote me, but Mr. Loyd continued blandly, "McCall put up the money and so did I, and then he spent thirty minutes of his valuable time tugging at that 'toy.' In the end, I pocketed his dollars and remarked, 'Mr. McCall, I'll take that off for you if you'll agree to take out a ten-thousand-dollar policy on your life.' He laughed. 'Great!' he said. 'This will make folks remember our agents!' That was one of my most successful puzzles. Now you take it off."

The thing looked so silly that I tried. I pushed and pulled and nearly tore my buttonhole out, but in vain. Sam Loyd smiled and smiled and refused to help. Finally, I gave it up, and the foolish thing dangled from my coat for the rest of the interview, which was just then interrupted by the entrance of a dapper young fellow, a drummer from a bond house. . . .

Near the end of the interview Loyd explained:

"It seems to me puzzle practice is a valuable help in waking up children's minds. . . . I think that I've made many a boy interested in mathematics or engineering who otherwise would have abhorred them. Vanity in an old man is not becoming so I won't say that I consider myself as something of an educator of American youth. But, if I did so consider myself, I should be prouder of that distinction than of having been the inventor of 'Pigs in Clover' [a classic mechanical puzzle in which one tries to roll tiny balls into sockets] or having made a million dollars—if I had made a million dollars."

"Right you see!" I cried enthusiastically, slapping my note-book shut. But with that motion my hand hit the foolish little toy night-stick dangling from my buttonhole. "Please, Mr. Loyd," I begged, "take this thing off."

"No," he smiled, "*you* take it off. It's very easy."

So I left the dingy office where Sam Loyd sat amid the litter of ten thousand puzzles, took the dingy elevator and walked up the dingy side street to Broadway. And at the corner I met the dapper young bond-broker. As he hastened by he looked superciliously at the toy dangling from my buttonhole. I whipped out my knife and cut it off! I'm too old to be educated. [The key to removing the dangling toy can be discerned from the "Coffee Break" puzzle in chapter 14.]

Before he was ten, Loyd invented several charming puzzles. One of his first brain benders (diagram 8-1) concerns three men who live in a common courtyard but leave the yard through different gates. Each man exits through the gate opposite his house. After the men have a falling-out, each builds an enclosed path to his gate. None of the paths crosses. How do the men accomplish this? (The artwork in this chapter—with the exception of diagrams 8-2, 8-3, 8-6, 8-7, 8-8, 8-11 and 8-18—originally appeared with Loyd's puzzles. Many of the illustrations were probably drawn by Loyd himself.)

When Loyd was fourteen, his first chess problem was published, in the *New York Saturday Courier* (diagram 8-2). By the age of twenty, he had earned a reputation as the greatest chess-problem composer in the history of the game; Wilhelm Stein-

8-1

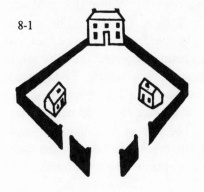

8-2
White to mate in three.

itz, the world chess champion from 1866 till 1894, offered the highest praise: "If a man wanted to solve one of Loyd's problems by analyzing every possible move he would naturally get the solution, but only on his last trial—not before."

In 1859, when Loyd was seventeen, he composed the Famous Trick Donkeys puzzle (diagram 8-3), which earned him ten thousand dollars in a few weeks; reportedly, a billion of these puzzles were sold during his lifetime. The object was to rearrange three drawings, two of a donkey and one of two jockeys, so that the jockeys were riding on the donkeys' backs. At the time Famous Trick Donkeys was released, Loyd was planning to become an engineer, but the puzzle's commercial success led him to make a career of enigmatic activity. Forty-three years later Loyd, in the interview in *Delineator*, put it this way: "If you could make ten thousand dollars in fifteen minutes with a puzzle, would you stick to engineering?"

During the Civil War Loyd achieved his second puzzle success. He went to Europe with his father, who was trying to raise money for the United States government by selling war bonds abroad. On the return voyage Loyd met Andrew Curtin, the Governor of Pennsylvania. The two of them got into a discussion about the thousand-year-old White Horse Monument on Uffington Hill in Berkshire, England. The monument consists of a huge horse, visible from miles away, carved out of the side of the hill. Curtain suggested that the white horse might provide the inspiration for a puzzle. Loyd immediately took up the suggestion, and in a few minutes he had created The Pony Puzzle: the silhouette of an old nag, cut out of black paper (diagram 8-4). The idea was to figure out how to rearrange the six pieces of the black nag on a white background, such as a sheet of white paper, to form the outline of a white horse. Try it!

Loyd patented and copyrighted many of his puzzles, although he was unable to take out a patent on one of his most famous creations, The 14–15 Puzzle, or Boss Puzzle (diagram

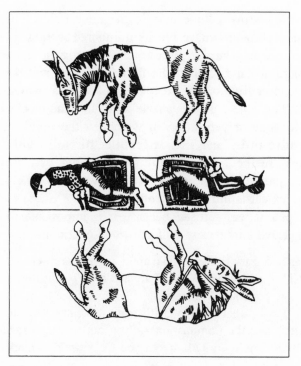

8-3

8-4

The Pony Puzzle

8-5), which drove people mad in the early 1870s. The puzzle consists of fifteen square blocks numbered from 1 to 15 that are arranged in a large square frame. Initially the sixteenth, or bottom right-hand, cell in the frame is empty and the blocks are in consecutive order except for 14 and 15, which are reversed. The object of the puzzle is to slide the blocks around so as to achieve a position in which *all* the numbers are in consecutive order and the sixteenth cell is still blank. Before you read further, I urge you to figure out why Loyd was denied a patent on this puzzle. An easy way to try the puzzle is with index cards numbered from 1 to 15.

The patent was refused because it is impossible to do the puzzle! Loyd's interview in The *Strand* continues:

> It was necessary to file with an application for a patent a "working model" of the device. When I applied for a patent they asked me if it was possible to change the relations of the fourteen and fifteen. I said that it was mathematically impossible to do so. "Then," said the Commissioner, "you can't have a patent. For if the thing won't work, how can you file a working model of it?"

8-5

His logic was all right, and the result was that I didn't get my patent.

In spite of that, however, there are thousands of persons in the United States who believe they solved that puzzle. I was talking with my shoemaker the other day, when a big Irishman, sitting not far away, who had overheard us, said, "Are ye the mon that invinted th' Fourteen-Fifteen puzzle? I did that puzzle." I laughed, and said that couldn't be, because it couldn't be done. "Don't you say I didn't do it," he replied, "or I'll flatten the nose on y'r face." He was a pretty big man, and I suppose he could have done it, too. Yes, there were many thousands of persons who were sure they had done it; but the thousand dollars reward I offered for anyone who would do it was never claimed. Not long ago the Sunday editor of a New York paper wanted to use it again as a supplement, and I suggested he should offer a thousand dollars reward for the solution. He refused. He said he remembered very well that he had done the puzzle once, and he wasn't going to throw away a thousand dollars. Before I could persuade him to offer the reward, I had to bring the thousand dollars to his office and deposit it in the safe. It was never claimed.

The mathematics behind the puzzle is straightforward. If the problem is solvable, the route the blank cell takes is a round trip. Any such route entails the cyclical permutation of an odd number of blocks. Suppose the blank takes the shortest possible circular route (diagram 8-6), through positions twelve, eleven and fifteen. (Do not confuse the positions in the frame with the numbers on the blocks.) In that case, the three blocks 11, 12 and 14 have been cyclically rearranged. Any cyclical rearrangement could be achieved, if the rules of the puzzle allowed, by simply interchanging pairs of blocks. The new arrangement of blocks 11, 12 and 14 could have been reached by two simple interchanges: 11 for 12 and then 12 for 14. It turns out that the cyclical permutation of an odd number of blocks is always equivalent to an even number of simple interchanges. (The result can be expressed even more generally: in combinatorial

1	2	3	4
5	6	7	8
9	10	14	11
13	15	12	

8-6

mathematics it is known that the cyclical permutation of n objects is the same as $n-1$ simple interchanges.) Therefore, the round-trip movement of the blank cell entails an even number of simple interchanges.

In the initial configuration of the blocks, one simple interchange (15 for 14) must be effected in order to solve the puzzle. This cannot be achieved because the desired position can be brought about only by an even number of simple interchanges.

When Loyd was not in a mischievous mood, he posed three problems that could be solved, given the initial arrangement of the blocks:

1. Shift the blocks away so that they are in consecutive order, but with the vacant square in the top left corner instead of the bottom right (diagram 8-7).
2. Rotate the frame 90 degrees clockwise. Then put the blocks in consecutive order, with the vacant square in the bottom right corner (diagram 8-8).
3. Move the blocks until they form a magic square, the blocks adding up to 30 in ten different directions.

Even without a patent Loyd made money from The 14–15 Puzzle. But he was not always that lucky. According to his

	1	2	3
4	5	6	7
8	9	10	11
12	13	14	15

8-7

1	2	3	4
5	6	7	8
9	10	11	12
13	14	15	

8-8

own account, he invented the game Parcheesi, for a company that had a huge quantity of multicolored cardboard it didn't know what to do with. The company asked Loyd to suggest some use for the cardboard, and on the spot he dreamed up Parcheesi. "How much do we owe you?" the head of the concern asked. Loyd explained that he didn't want any money because it had taken him only a few seconds to think up the game. But the man insisted on giving him ten dollars—for a game that soon netted millions for the company. The reason that Parcheesi is not commonly thought of as his creation but as an ancient game, Loyd claims, is that he himself had told too well a story about a missionary who found heathens playing it in eastern India. (Loyd's claim, however, is bunk.)

Deprived of profits from Parcheesi, Loyd still was not suffering. Many of his contemporaries claimed he was a millionaire, although Loyd steadfastly denied this—noting that he didn't know how much he made from puzzles because he didn't keep financial records. It is clear, however, that he was a man of considerable means.

Although Loyd received next to nothing for Parcheesi, he was generally able to command a lot of money for his puzzles and games—and was obsessed with doing so. He told the *Strand:*

I have received salaries of twenty-five to one hundred dollars a
week from several papers at the same time for conducting their
puzzle departments. Besides, I have a big source of profits in the
letters I receive . . . sometimes one hundred thousand letters a
day. I have a corps of clerks to go over them and pick out,
possibly, a thousand that I ought to see personally. But the letters
I sell because the addresses and names are valuable. Two days ago
I sold a lot of one hundred thousand letters to a mail order house
for one hundred and twenty dollars, and the next day I sold a
Sunday newspaper another lot at one dollar a thousand—one hundred dollars. That isn't a bad addition to one's income.

Loyd's favorite puzzle, released in 1896, was called Get Off
the Earth, or Chinaman. William McKinley distributed the
puzzle as a promotional gag in his successful presidential cam-
paign that year. (Some of the appeal of the puzzle was unfortunately the result of its tapping America's widespread fear of
Oriental immigration.)

Unfortunately [recalled Loyd in 1907], it came out in a bad year
and did not achieve the success of some of the others. But I am
going to revive it, and there is no doubt it will equal their success.
It was developed under rather odd conditions. My son—who
thinks I can do anything—said to me one morning, "Here's a
chance for you to earn two hundred and fifty dollars, pop," and
he threw a newspaper clipping across the breakfast table. It was an
offer by Percy Williams of two hundred and fifty dollars for the
best device for advertising Bergen Beach, which he was about to
open as a pleasure resort. I said I'd take a chance at it, and a few
days later I had worked out the Chinaman puzzle [diagram 8-9]. It
was two pieces of card, which were fastened together so that they
moved on a pivot. As you looked at them there were thirteen
Chinamen plainly pictured [clinging to the surface of the Earth].
Move the cards together a little and there were twelve perfect
Chinamen. You couldn't tell what had become of the other Chinaman, try as you would. Scientists have tried to solve it without
success. Oh, yes; there is a solution, but I sha'n't tell what it is.

Before

After

8-9

Loyd was fond of Get Off the Earth because it involved vanishing—a theme repeated in many of his puzzles. In his 1909 creation Teddy and the Lions, a circular piece of cardboard is mounted on a pivot to a larger, rectangular piece. Theodore Roosevelt, who was known for his African safaris, seven Africans, and seven lions are drawn across the two pieces. When the circular piece is slightly rotated, a man is seen to vanish, but not Teddy.

The vanishing motif is also found in Loyd's puzzle Sailing under False Colors (diagram 8-10). Loyd noted that on May 1, 1795, two stripes were added to the original thirteen-stripe American flag because two new states, Vermont and Kentucky, had joined the Union. The practice of having the number of stripes on the flag reflect the number of states was curtailed by a Congressional resolution in 1817 that restored the flag to its original thirteen stripes but stipulated that a star should be added for each new state. Not one to tolerate waste, Loyd posed the problem of converting the fifteen-stripe flag into a thirteen-stripe flag without discarding *any* material. See if you can figure out how to divide the flag of fifteen stripes

8-10

into the fewest pieces that will fit together to form the flag of thirteen stripes.

In each of the three puzzles—Get Off the Earth, Teddy and the Lions and Sailing under False Colors—the missing elements reappear when everything is shifted back to the way it was originally. In that sense, the theme of these puzzles is as much spontaneous creation as it is disappearance. Indeed, if you were first shown the final setup and then the initial one, the question would be: How did the Chinaman or the African or the two stripes appear out of thin air? The act of counterfeiting by creating an extra bill from existing ones is just another case of the vanishing motif in reverse. (Gardner's *Mathematics, Magic and Mystery* contains a wonderful discussion of the many guises the vanishing paradox can take.)

The vanishing paradox can be resolved by reducing it to its essentials. Consider six rectangles lined up in a row (diagram 8-11a). I am going to cut off one-fifth of the second rectangle and add it to the first, cut off two-fifths of the third rectangle and add it to what remains of the second, cut off three-fifths of the fourth rectangle and add it to what remains of the third, cut off four-fifths of the fifth rectangle and add it to what remains of the fourth, and take the sixth rectangle and add it to what remains of the fifth. (Diagram 8-11b should make this clear.)

The paradox of creation can be disposed of by the same diagram. Consider the five rectangles in (b). The idea is to cut them along the lines indicated and then reassemble the pieces to form the six rectangles in (a). The rectangles in (a) are five-sixths the length of those in (b). In other words, in the process of creating a new rectangle, each of the original ones is shortened by a sixth.

Now, imagine that the five rectangles in (b) are five one-dollar bills. They can be converted into six by the above method. Some manual dexterity is required to glue together the pieces of the bills in such a way as to minimize seams. The

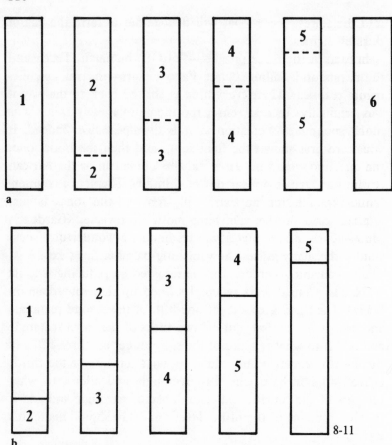

8-11

more bills used, the better. That way, each bill loses a smaller fraction of its length. If n bills are used, each bill is shortened by an $(n+1)$th of its length.

The Cambridge policeman cited by *The Harvard Crimson* apparently did not understand the mechanics of this system of counterfeiting. It is hard to imagine how ten bills could be converted into twelve, each a quarter of an inch shorter than normal, as he reported. However, by the procedure I've outlined, eleven bills can be made into twelve, each of which is half an inch shorter than normal.

Loyd died in 1911 of progressive apoplexy, and his son, who was also named Sam, took over his father's puzzle columns. Three years later he privately published *Cyclopedia of Puzzles*, a mammoth collection of his father's work. The following problems are from the *Cyclopedia*, and they show that Loyd, Sr., had great range in his enigmatic activity.

Like many other great enigmatologists, Loyd had a fatal weakness for painfully bad riddles. Why is a sick Hebrew like an emerald? Because he is a Jew ill. When are there but twenty-five letters in the alphabet? When *U* and *I* are one. (A child told me a modern version of this riddle: Why does the alphabet have only twenty-two letters? Because *J.R.* was shot and *E.T.* went home) At what time in his life may a man be said to belong to a vegetable kingdom? When long experience has made him sage.

Not all of his riddling was inane. He came up with some clever stuff, which I offer to you in the form of problems.

UNSOLVED RIDDLE:

Probably everyone of the millions upon millions of people who have enjoyed Lewis Carroll's masterly and realistic description of the vagaries which flit through our minds while in dreamland have pondered over certain unanswered conundrums which were given by Alice in Wonderland. While Alice, the Mad March Hare and the crazy Hatter were enjoying their tea, the Hatter suggested some riddles and asked, "Why is a writing desk like a raven?" Alice said she believed she could guess it, but every time the question was repeated it flitted from her mind and faded away like that mysterious cat, which left nothing more tangible than its everlasting smile. It is safe to assume, however, that the famous Oxford mathematician and noted puzzlist had some clever answer up his sleeve, or he would not have proposed the conundrum. [What did Loyd think Carroll had in mind?]

THE PLAYERS WHO ALL WON:

As an improvement upon the accepted notion that winners can only gain as much as the losers lose, I take occasion to call attention to a more profitable style of play, of which it is narrated:

Four jolly men sat down to play,
And played all night till break of day;
They played for gold and not for fun,
With separate scores for everyone.
Yet, when they came to square accounts,
They all had made quite fair amounts!
Can you the paradox explain?
If no one lost, how could all gain?

Loyd's fascination with wordplay extended far beyond riddles. Here are two examples.

MISSING-WORD ANAGRAM:

Use a four-letter word, the same letters each time, in each of the blank spaces, and make good sense of the following rhyme:

A _____ old woman on _____ bent
Put on her _____ and away she went;
_____ she cried, as she went on her way,
How are we going to _____ today?

POETICAL DECAPITATIONS:

Here is an odd little bit of decapitation, where the removal of the first letter, then the second, third and fourth in the three missing words, makes the meaning clear:

The lilies on the bank are _____ ,
While in our little bark we're _____
Our course to favoring breezes _____ ,
Like birds upon the _____ .

With lily-pads the oars are _____ ,
As eager hands the blossoms _____ ;
Each shouts "Dull care away _____ ,"
And echo answers " _____ ."

It seems to me a strange _____ ,
That we should pay so great _____ ,
For trifles like a little _____ ,
Or such a common thing as _____ .

Mathematical puzzles were Loyd's forte, particularly those that involved cutting up objects.

THE PATCH QUILT PUZZLE:

The sketch [diagram 8-12] represents the members of the "Willing Workers" society overwhelming their good parson with a token of love and esteem, in the shape of a beautiful patchwork quilt. Every member contributed one square piece of patchwork consisting of one or more or the small squares, each of these contributions being perfectly square in shape, involving a pretty puzzle which nearly disrupted the society.

Any lady would have resigned if her particular piece of work

8-12

was tampered with or omitted, so it became a matter of considerable study to find out how to unite all of the squares of various
sizes together so as to form the one large square quilt. Incidentally
it may be mentioned that as every member contributed one square
piece of quilt, you will know just how many members there were
when you discover into how few square pieces the quilt can be
divided. It is a simple puzzle which will give considerable scope
for ingenuity and patience.

CROSS AND CRESCENT:

Here is a pretty and scientific puzzle closely allied to Hypocrates' famous mathematical problem of the relation of a square to a lune. The problem in this case being to discover how to convert the crescent into the form of a Greek cross, as shown upon the goddess's head, by cutting the moon into the fewest possible number of pieces which can be fitted together so as to form a cross [diagram 8-13].

The routing of a vehicle or a person from one place to another was a common theme in Loyd's puzzles. Loyd was happiest when he could combine the routing motif with one of his great loves, the railroad.

THE SWITCH PROBLEM:

This is a practical problem of railroad men, given to illustrate some of the complications of everyday affairs, and is based upon reminiscences of the days when railroading was in its infancy, before the introduction of double tracks, turn tables or automatic switches. Yet I am not going back to the days of our great-grand-fathers, for there are those among us who are familiar with the advent of the iron horse, and the good lady who furnished me with the subject matter of this puzzle based it upon personal experience of what she called "the other day."

To tell the story in her own way, she said: "We had just arrived at the switch station, where the trains always pass, when we found that the Lincoln Express had broken down. I think the conductor man said that the smokestack had got hot and collapsed, so there was no draught to pull it off the track."

The picture [diagram 8-14] shows the Limited Express, with its collapsed engine, and the approach of the accommodation train from Wayback, which, by some means or other, must pass the stalled train. The problem being to make the two trains pass, it is understood that no ropes, poles, flying switches and so on are to

8-14

be employed; it is a switch puzzle pure and simple, the object being to put the accommodation train past the wreck and leave the latter train and each of its cars in the position as shown in the sketch. It is necessary to say that there is but room enough for one car or engine on the sections of the switch marked *A, B, C* or *D*.

The problem is to tell just how many times the engineer must reverse; that is, change the direction of the engine to perform the feat. Of course the broken down engine cannot be used as a motor, but must be pushed or pulled along just as if it was a car. The cars may be drawn singly or coupled together in any required numbers.

The problem complies with the ordinary rules of practice and is given to test your ingenuity and cleverness in discovering the quickest possible way to pass the broken down train.

Sometimes Loyd's puzzles were so novel that they had no precedent—whether in his own work or in that of his paradoxical forebears. Here is a case in point.

THE GREAT COLUMBUS PROBLEM:

I recently came across a vividly written description of the fif-
teenth-century craze for gambling, wherein among other games of
skill or chance upon which the cavaliers were wont to bet so
recklessly, mention was made of the sport of laying eggs upon a
cloth. Here possibly was the true solution to the Columbus egg
story, which despite its clever moral has always seemed too tame
for such a fierce period. I saw that there was a pretty principle
involved and present it as a clever souveneer [sic] of the fifteenth
century, which differs from ordinary tricks and puzzles in that it
calls for ingenious and original lines of thought instead of experimental methods. As a matter of fact, in place of a practical demonstration, our puzzlists are merely called upon to exercise their wits
in suggesting the best theory or principle whereby to solve the
problem, for a clever person should guess the puzzle from the
picture [diagram 8-15].

It is simply a game played between two opponents placing eggs
alternatively upon a square napkin in order to see who can win by
placing the last egg. After an egg is placed it must not be moved

8-15

or touched by another one, but as the size of the napkin or the eggs, as well as the variable distances which may occur between them, is of no importance, it would look as if the question of placing the last egg was a matter of luck or chance, and yet the winning trick, as the great navigator remarked, "is the easiest thing in the world when you are shown how!"

ANSWERS

8-16

Diagram 8-16 shows how each man connected his house to his gate.

Loyd's first chess problem is solved by 1. R–B8 check QxR 2. Q–Q6 check RxQ 3. N–K5 mate.

The Pony Puzzle is solved by rearranging the pieces of the black horse to form the outline of the white pony as shown in diagram 8-17.

8-17

13	1	6	10
14	2	5	9
	12	11	7
3	15	8	4

8-18

The three problems about The 14–15 Puzzle can be solved as follows, where a cited number means that that number is moved into the blank cell. The first position can be achieved in forty-four moves: 14, 11, 12, 8, 7, 6, 10, 12, 8, 7, 4, 3, 6, 4, 7, 14, 11, 15, 13, 9, 12, 8, 4, 10, 8, 4, 14, 11, 15, 13, 9, 12, 4, 8, 5, 4, 8, 9, 13, 14, 10, 6, 2 and 1. The second position can be reached in thirty-nine moves: 14, 15, 10, 6, 7, 11, 15, 10, 13, 9, 5, 1, 2, 3, 4, 8, 12, 15, 10, 13, 9, 5, 1, 2, 3, 4, 8, 12, 15, 14, 13, 9, 5, 1, 2, 3, 4, 8 and 12. The third position, the magic square (diagram 8-18), can be achieved in fifty moves: 12, 8, 4, 3, 2, 6, 10, 9, 13, 15, 14, 12, 8, 4, 7, 10, 9, 14, 12, 8, 4, 7, 10, 9, 6, 2, 3, 10, 9, 6, 5, 1, 2, 3, 6, 5, 3, 2, 1, 13, 14, 3, 2, 1, 13, 14, 3, 12, 15 and 3. Every row, column and principal diagonal adds up to 30.

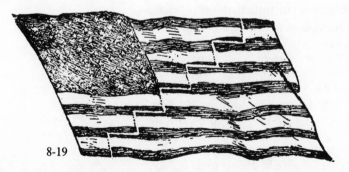

8-19

In Sailing under False Colors, only one cut (diagram 8–19) will make the fifteen-stripe flag a thirteen-stripe flag!

UNSOLVED RIDDLE: Why is a raven like a writing desk? Loyd thought that they are similar "because the notes for which they are noted are not noted for being musical notes." Scott Garland, of West Bloomfield, Michigan, recently came up with another clever solution: "Because Edgar Allan Poe wrote on both of them."

THE PLAYERS WHO ALL WON: "The players who all won were fiddlers in the German band and gained $5 per night. I did not intimate they were card players."

MISSING-WORD ANAGRAM: The key word is *vile*.

A *vile* old woman on *evil* bent
Put on her *veil* and away she went;
Levi she cried as she went on her way,
How are we going to *live* today?

POETICAL DECAPITATION: The key words are *growing, trifling* and *caprice*.

The lilies on the bank are *growing*,
While in our little bark we're *rowing*
Our course to favoring breezes *owing*,
Like birds upon the *wing*.

With lily-pads the oars are *trifling*.
As eager hands the blossoms *rifling*;
Each shouts "Dull care away *I fling*,"
And echo answers "*Fling*."

It seems to me a strange *caprice*,
That we should pay so great *a price*,
For trifles like a little *rice*,
Or such a common thing as *ice*.

THE PATCH QUILT PUZZLE: Diagram 8-20 shows how the 13×13 quilt can be divided into eleven smaller squares, which is the least number of square pieces it will divide into without destroying the checkered pattern. It proved to be a difficult puzzle, and those who discovered the correct answer found that there was a certain mathematical principle involved, which held them close to the rules of square root.

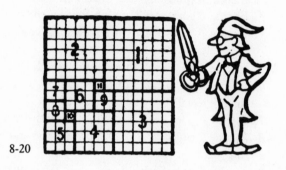

8-20

8-21

CROSS AND CRESCENT: "The crescent can be divided into six pieces as shown, when by turning over one piece they will form the cross [diagram 8-21]."

THE SWITCH PROBLEM: Think of the train cars as being numbered from 1 to 9, starting on the left. That makes the stalled engine 5 and the working engine 6. The solution calls for engine 6 to reverse direction thirty-one times.

1. Engine 6 leaves its train and passes through the switch via the sections of track marked C, B and A (one reversal).
2. Engine 6 pulls engine 5 to section D of the track (one reversal).
3. Engine 6 goes back through the switch (two reversals).
4. Engine 6 pulls car 4 to D, pushing engine 5 to the right (one reversal).
5. Engine 6 goes back through the switch (two reversals).
6. Engine 6 pulls car 3 to D, pushing 4 and 5 farther to the right (one reversal).
7. Engine 6 goes back through the switch (two reversals).
8. Engine 6 pulls car 2 to D, pushing 3, 4 and 5 farther to the right (one reversal).
9. Engine 6 goes back through the switch (two reversals).
10. Engine 6 pulls car 1 to D, pushing 2, 3, 4 and 5 farther to the right (one reversal).
11. Engine 6 now goes through the switch for the last time (two reversals)!
12. Cars 1, 2, 3, 4, 5 and 7 are hooked together, and engine 6 draws train 123457 to the left (one reversal).
13. Engine 6 starts to back train 123457 onto the switch, leaving car 7 on section A (one reversal).
14. Engine 6 pulls train 12345 to the left and then pushes the train to the right (two reversals).
15. Engine 6 goes alone to the left, backs up onto A and pulls car 7 to the left (three reversals).
16. Engine 6 backs car 7 onto train 12345, which is then hooked to cars 8 and 9 (one reversal).
17. Engine 6 pulls the whole shebang to the left (one reversal).
18. Engine 6 backs the train 71234589 onto the switch, leaving cars 8 and 9 on A and B, respectively (one reversal).

19. Engine 6 pulls 712345 to the left and backs 712345 to the right (two reversals).
20. Engine 6 pulls car 7 alone to the left and then backs car 7 into cars 8 and 9 (two reversals).
21. Now train 6789 is able to move to the left, while train 12345 waits on the right for its engine to be repaired (one reversal).

THE GREAT COLUMBUS PROBLEM:

The secret of winning in a contest to see who can place the last egg upon a square napkin, as described in the Columbus puzzle, turns upon placing the first egg exactly in the center of the napkin [diagram 8-22]. Then, no matter where your opponent places an egg, duplicate his play on the opposite in a direct line through egg No. 1. The numbers given illustrate the beginning of the game,

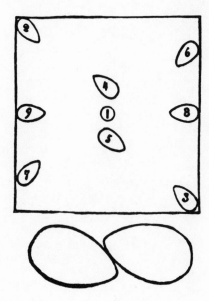

8-22

proceeding in regular order of play, viz.: 1, 2, 3, 4, 5, 6, 7, 8, 9 and so on.

The placing of the first egg would not win if simply laid on the table, for, owing to the oval form of the egg, the second player might place an egg in close proximity to the conical end, as shown below the square diagram, which could not be duplicated.

The only way to win, therefore, as discovered by the great navigator, according to popular history, is to flatten one end of the [first] egg played so as to make it stand erect, so as to represent a circle [as you look down on the egg].

This puzzle, as previously explained, was not given for practical demonstration, but just to develop the gray matter in the brain.

Loyd neglected to mention that all the eggs must be the same size, although that can be any size at all.

9

Call Me a Cab, or the History of the (Fatal) Riddle

The riddle was once the most literary form of puzzle. Poets wrote them, as did philosophers, scientists and spurned lovers. Great statesmen have also resorted to them in order to win political arguments. When a Confederate sympathizer told Abraham Lincoln that the blacks in the South were not enslaved but "protected," the President responded with a riddle: "How many legs will a sheep have if you call a tail a leg?" "Five," replied Lincoln's adversary. "Four," said the President, "for calling a tail a leg does not make it one."

In a speech to Congress in 1806 about a much-violated act that forbade trading with other countries, Josiah Quincy said:

They who introduced it abjured it. They who advocated it did not wish, and scarcely knew, its use. And now that it is said to be extended over us, no man in this nation, who values his reputation, will take his Bible oath that it is in effectual and legal operation. There is an old riddle on a coffin, which I presume we all learned when we were boys, that it is as perfect a representation of the origin, progress, and present state of this thing called non-intercourse, as it is possible to be conceived:

There was a man bespoke a thing,
Which when the maker home did bring,
That same maker did refuse it,
The man that spoke for it did not use it,
And he who had it did not know
Whether he had it, yea or no.

True it is that if this non-intercourse shall ever be, in reality, subtended over us, the similitude will fall in a material point. The poor tenant of the coffin is ignorant of his state. But the people of the United States will be literally buried alive in non-intercourse, and realize the grave closing on themselves and on their hopes, with a full and cruel consciousness of all the horrors of their condition.

Today, children have displaced the politicos and the literati as the chief composers of riddles. Why is getting up at 5:00 a.m. like a pig's tail? It's twirly. What will go up a chimney down, but won't go down a chimney up? An umbrella. Why did the tuna blush? It saw the salad dressing. What's Irish and is put outside in the summer? Patio furniture.

Even Lincoln's wordplay has been preserved in a juvenile way. How many times has the directive "Call me a cab" been met by the response "You're a cab"?

Riddles, like magic squares, are rooted in antiquity. The Bible is riddled with them. The Book of Judges of the Old Testament includes a tragic example of the ancient custom of telling riddles at nuptial celebrations. At his wedding banquet, Samson posed the riddle: "Out of the eater came forth meat, and out of the strong came forth sweetness." He offered a prize of thirty garments and thirty bed sheets to anyone who solved it within seven days. No one was able to solve it legitimately because it was based on something extraordinary that Samson had seen and described only to his wife: the stomach of a lion he had slaughtered had housed a swarm of bees. The wedding guests coerced Samson's bride into telling them the answer. When they told it to Samson, he went on a rampage and killed his wife and thousands of Philistines. Although Samson may have overreacted, his riddle is one of many historically important ones that had fatal consequences.

People who have solved riddles have been amply rewarded, whereas those who have failed to answer them correctly have suffered—often fatally. Ancient Thebes was plagued by the Sphinx, who posed a famous riddle to all who passed her: "What walks on four legs in the morning, on two legs at noon and on three legs in the evening?" The Sphinx slew everyone who could not solve the riddle. Oedipus eventually saved the city by providing the answer: "Man. As a baby, he crawls on all fours. As an adult, he stands erect. And as an old man, he makes use of a cane." After Oedipus solved the riddle, the Sphinx threw herself off a cliff and Oedipus was crowned King of Thebes.

Legend has it that Homer worried himself to death pondering a riddle that a fisherman posed: "What I caught I left behind. What I brought I didn't find. What was the catch?" The answer was fleas.

Not all ancient riddles had grave consequences. In Athens the telling of riddles was a customary way of unwinding from serious discourse. The Athenian who solved a riddle was rewarded with a garland and the applause of the company. The punishment for an incorrect answer was to drink, without taking a breath, a cup of wine mixed with salt.

As early as the sixteenth century riddles were expressed in verse. *The Booke of Merry Riddles,* which Shakespeare mentions in *The Merry Wives of Windsor,* gave several riddles in verse, of which I quote two:

1

Ten fish I caught without an eye.
And nine without a tail;
Six had no head, and half of eight
I weighed upon the scale;
Now who can tell me as I ask it,
How many fish were in my basket?

2

He went to the wood and caught it,
He sate him downe and sought it;
Because he could not find it,
Home with him he brought it.

The answer to the first riddle is 0 (none). A 10 without a 1 is
0, a 9 without a tail is 0, a 6 without a head is 0, and so on.
The answer to the second riddle is a thorn. "For a man went
to the wood and caught a thorne in his foot, and then he sate
him down, and sought to have pulled it out, and because he
could not find it out, he must needs bring it home."

The first riddle in *The Booke of Merry Riddles,* which is in
prose, picks up on the leg motif introduced by the Sphinx:
"Two legs sate upon three legs, and had one leg in her hand;
then in came foure legs, and bare away one leg; then up start
two legs, and threw three legs at foure legs, and brought again
one leg." Ponder this awhile before you read on.

Ready for the answer? "A woman with two legs sate on a
stoole with three legs, and has a leg of mutton in her hand;
then came a dog that hath foure legs, and bare away the leg of
mutton; then up start the woman, and threw the stool with
three legs at the dog with foure legs, and brought again the leg
of mutton."

Kids have also responded to the leg motif. What has eighteen legs and two breasts? Answer: The Supreme Court.

In England riddles and related word puzzles flourished in
the eighteenth and nineteenth centuries. My favorite is one

that Jonathan Swift, the author of *Gulliver's Travels*, first
heard in the early 1700s:

> Because I am by nature blind,
> I wisely choose to walk behind;
> However, to avoid disgrace,
> I let no creature see my face.
> My words are few, but spoke with sense;
> And yet my speaking gives offence:
> Or if to whisper I presume
> The company will fly the room.
> By all the world I am opprest:
> And my oppression gives them rest.

The answer is the posterior.

Swift also composed his own riddles, such as:

> We are little airy creatures,
> All of different voice and features;
> One of us in glass is set,
> One of us you'll find in jet,
> T'other you may see in tin,
> And the fourth a box within.
> If the fifth you should pursue,
> It can never fly from you.

The "little airy creatures" are the five voewels, *a, e, i, o* and *u*.

In the late eighteenth century an English work, *The Masquerade*, posed the riddle: "Why is a man who has seen a
young goat asleep likely to give an account of a stolen child?"
The answer is that he has witnessed the kid-napping. *The
Masquerade* also contains a riddle in verse:

> Pray tell me, ladies, if you can,
> Who is that highly favor'd man,
> Who, tho' he's married many a wife,
> May still live single all his life?

The answer is a clergyman.

Letters of the alphabet are often the answers to riddles. Witness the following from *The Puzzling Cap: Being a Choice Collection of Riddles*, published in London in 1813:

> I'm found in most countries, yet not in earth or sea,
> I am in all timber, yet not in any tree,
> I am in all metals, yet I am told,
> I am not in lead, iron, brass, silver or gold,
> I am not in England, yet this I can say,
> I'm to be found in Westmister every day.

The answer, of course, is the letter *m*.

Most books of riddles published in the nineteenth century were written under a pseudonym or cited no author at all. For example, in 1834 *The Phoenix, or, a Choice Collection of Riddles and Charades*, by Peter Puzzlewell, Esq., was published in London. The book includes a riddle ("What is that which is in the constant possession of every human being; which cannot be bought, yet has been sold: it is invisible—never seen, but often felt?") the answer to which also fits a long riddle in a book published in Dublin in 1799, *Christmas Amusement; or, the Happy Association of Mirth and Ingenuity: Being an Elegant Collection of Original Riddles, Charades, etc. Culled from the Vase of Fancy at Conundrum Castle*, by Peregrine Puzzlebrains:

> Without my aid no mortal can survive,
> Yet I'm unknown to those I keep alive;
> By me, they move, and speak, and challenge fame,
> Yet none of them did ever see my frame.
> I am the greatest friend that mortals know,
> All other times I am a potent foe.
> Yet while you read the vast immensity,
> Vain is your greatest art, if turn'd on me.
> Most authors term me of the female kind,

For they're the brightest works by Heav'n design'd;
Yet one advantage doth to me belong,
Their beauties fade, but I am ever young.

The answer is the soul.

In the middle of the nineteenth century Lewis Carroll extended the tradition of posing riddles in verse by answering them that way, too. Here are two of his cleverest:

1

John gave his brother James a box:
About it there were many locks.

James woke and said it gave him pain:
So gave it back to John again.

The box was not with lid supplied,
Yet caused two lids to open wide:

And all these locks had never a key—
What kind of box, then, could it be?

2

Three sisters at breakfast were feeding the cat,
The first gave it sole—Puss was grateful for that:
The next gave it salmon—which Puss thought a treat:
The third gave it herring—which Puss wouldn't eat.
[Explain the conduct of the cat.]

Carroll gave as the answers:

1

As curly-headed Jemmy was sleeping in bed,
His brother John gave him a blow on the head;
James opened his eyelids, and spying his brother,
Doubled his fist and gave him another.
This kind of box then is not so rare;
The lids are the eyelids, the locks are the hair,

And so every schoolboy can tell to his cost,
The key to the tangles is constantly lost.

2

That salmon and sole Puss should think very grand
Is no such remarkable thing.
For more of these dainties Puss took up her stand;
But when the third sister stretched out her fair hand
Pray why should Puss swallow her ring?

It is not uncommon for people to offer cash prizes for the answers to unsolved riddles. I want to close this chapter with two classic examples, which appeared in my column in *Science Digest*. Afterward, I'll share with you the solutions that readers sent me.

The will of Miss Anna Seward, an eighteenth-century poet who was a friend of Darwin's grandfather and was known as the Swan of Lichfield, contained a riddlelike puzzle and directions to pay £50 to the person who solved it. The lines have been numbered for purposes of discussion:

(1) The noblest object in the works of art
(2) The brightest scenes which nature can impart;
(3) The well-known signal in the time of peace,
(4) The point essential in a tenant's lease;
(5) The farmer's comfort as he drives the plough,
(6) A soldier's duty, and a lover's vow;
(7) A contract made before the nuptial tie,
(8) A blessing riches never can supply;
(9) A spot that adds new charms to pretty faces.
(10) An engine used in fundamental cases;
(11) A planet seen between the earth and sun,
(12) A prize that merit never yet has won;
(13) A loss which prudence seldom can retrieve,
(14) The death of Judas and the fall of Eve;
(15) A part between the ankle and the knee,

(16) A papist's toast, and a physician's fee;
(17) A wife's ambition, and a parson's dues,
(18) A miser's idol, and the badge of Jews.
(19) If now your happy genius can divine
(20) The correspondent words in every line,
(21) By the first letter plainly may be found
(22) An ancient city that is much renowned.

The Bishop of Salisbury offered a mere £15 to the person who solved this riddle:

(1) I sit alone on a rock
(2) Whilst I'm raising the wind,
(3) But the storm once abated
(4) I'm gentle and kind.
(5) I've kings at my feet
(6) Who await but my nod,
(7) To kneel down in the deep,
(8) On the ground that I've trod.
(9) Tho' oft seen by the world,
(10) I am known but to few;
(11) The gentiles despise me,
(12) I'm pork to the Jew.
(13) I never have passed
(14) But one night in the dark,
(15) And that was with Noah
(16) Alone in the Ark.
(17) My weight is three pounds,
(18) My length is a mile;
(19) And when I'm discovered
(20) You will say with a smile—
(21) That my first and my last
(22) Are the best of our isle.

James R. Snyder, of Wildwood, Illinois, was the first to send me a good solution to Seward's riddle. He first found words that answered to each couplet in the verse. Then he saw that the first letters of the words spell out *Bethlehem*. The words are *beauty* (lines 1 and 2), *elapse* (lines 3 and 4), *trust* (lines 5 and 6), *happiness* (lines 7 and 8), *lips* (lines 9 and 10), *elusive* (lines 11 and 12), *health* (lines 13 and 14), *enormous* (lines 15 and 16) and *money* (lines 17 and 18). Although I would quibble with a few of the words Snyder proposes (for example, in what sense is a papist's toast "enormous"?), I think the overall solution—Bethlehem—is the correct one.

Some seven hundred correspondents tried to justify, by lengthy and amusing arguments, a slew of answers to the Bishop's riddle, including a lighthouse, waves, the ocean, the Bible, the Christ Child, the devil, the Sirens, an idea, a snake, a seagull, a dove, a crow, a skunk, a milestone, the human hand, excrement, the letter *s* and sunshine. More than one person advanced ingenious arguments in favor of the answer *penis;* for example, the testicles are the rock on which the penis rests alone (line 1), the penis is soft and spent after ejaculation ("But the storm once abated / I'm gentle and kind"—lines 3 and 4), and "My length is a mile" (line 18) is a parody of the universal tendency of men to exaggerate the length of their penis.

The best answer suggested was *rainbow*, although I'm not entirely convinced that it is what the Bishop had in mind. The riddle mentions Noah and the Ark, and during the Great Flood the rainbow was God's signal to man that He would not destroy him again. "My weight is three pounds / My length is a mile" (lines 17 and 18), although not literally true of a rainbow, does get across that a rainbow is thin and long. Perhaps the "first" and "last" in line 21 are allusions to the first and last books of the Bible, Genesis and Revelation—the only places in the Bible where a rainbow is discussed.

10
The 4,600-Year-Long Lure of Magic Squares

Video games and mechanical puzzles such as Rubik's Cube have skyrocketed in popularity in recent years, but they have not displaced the simple crossword puzzle as the number-one form of enigmatic entertainment on this planet. Nearly 99 percent of all daily newspapers in the world—not just those in the United States—offer a crossword each day. Moreover, according to *What's Gnu?*, a delightful history of the crossword puzzle, in this country alone 677 Sunday newspapers carried a crossword in 1981. It is, however, a relatively recent invention; the first one appeared on December 21, 1913, in the "Fun" supplement to the Christmas issue of the *New York Sunday World* (diagram 10-1).

What, you may wonder, did people do to stretch their minds before they discovered the joy of putting letters in little boxes, one letter per box, to make interconnecting words? Well, for as many as 4,600 years before the invention of the crossword, people all over the globe derived inexplicable pleasure from putting numbers in little boxes, one number per box, to make interconnecting sums. This ancient form of puzzle is called a magic square; it consists of arranging a series

10-1
THE FIRST
CROSSWORD
PUZZLE

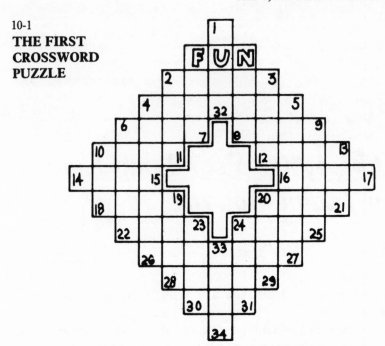

2-3. What bargain hunters enjoy.
4-5. A written acknowledgment.
6-7. Such and nothing more.
10-11. A bird.
14-15. Opposed to less.
18-19. What this puzzle is.
22-23. An animal of prey.
26-27. The close of a day.
28-29. To elude.
30-31. The plural of is.
8-9. To cultivate.
12-13. A bar of wood or iron.
16-17. What artists learn to do.
20-21. Fastened.
24-25. Found on the seashore.
10-18. The fibre of the gomuti palm.

6-22. What we all should be.
4-26. A day dream.
2-11. A talon.
19-28. A pigeon.
F-7. Part of your head.
23-30. A river in Russia.
1-32. To govern.
33-34. An aromatic plant.
N-8. A fist.
24-31. To agree with.
3-12. Part of a ship.
20-29. One.
5-27. Exchanging.
9-25. Sunk in mud.
13-21. A boy.

of consecutive numbers in a square in such a way that the sum of the numbers in each row and each column is the same. The sum is known as the pulse of the square. Ideally, the sum of the numbers in each of the two principal diagonals should also be equal to the pulse.

Diagram 10-2 shows a magic square concocted by none other than Benjamin Franklin. He included it in a letter to

10-2

BENJAMIN FRANKLIN'S SQUARE, 1750

52	61	4	13	20	29	36	45
14	3	62	51	46	35	30	19
53	60	5	12	21	28	37	44
11	6	59	54	43	38	27	22
55	58	7	10	23	26	39	42
9	8	57	56	41	40	25	24
50	63	2	15	18	31	34	47
16	1	64	49	48	33	32	17

Peter Collinson, a wealthy Quaker who sold his business to pursue botany, in about 1750. This square, whose pulse is 260, includes all the numbers from 1 to 64. The square is said to be of order eight because it is an eight-by-eight array of numbers. To appreciate how hard it is to construct a square of order eight, I urge you to try something much easier: make a magic square of order three from the numbers 1 through 9.

Such a square is the smallest one endowed with magic, and it has the configuration of a ticktacktoe board that has a border drawn around it (diagram 10-3). I forbid you to read further until you are able to make such a magic square.

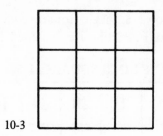

10-3

Magic squares have fascinated scientists, mathematicians, philosophers, theologians and astrologers, who see the numerical regularity as signaling a secret, underlying order in the universe. The magic square was apparently discovered in China, where in the fourth century B.C. the Chinese made much of the square of order three, called the Lo-Shu, whose numerical properties they interpreted as supporting the doctrines of Taoism.

Outside China, the earliest example of a magic square occurs in a Turkish manuscript written about A.D. 130. An Arabic treatise from A.D. 900 recommends that, to ensure a safe delivery, a pregnant woman should wear a charm inscribed with a magic square of order three.

Knowledge of the squares reached the Western world chiefly through the writings of Manuel Moschopoulos, a fourteenth-century Byzantine scholar. In the early sixteenth century Cornelius Agrippa, a German physician, published seven magic squares that he linked to the seven known "planets": sun, moon, Mars, Mercury, Jupiter, Venus and Saturn. Albrecht Dürer, the great German Renaissance artist who was Agrippa's contemporary, put a magic square of order four in his celebrated engraving *Melencolia I;* the two numbers in the middle of the square's bottom row (diagram 10-4) give the year of the engraving: 1514.

It was once thought that the magic square originated in India, but none can be reliably traced to earlier than the twelfth century A.D. Squares of order four were popular in India, and diagram 10-5 shows one of the earliest examples, with a pulse of 34, discovered in Khajuraho.

That a collection of consecutive numbers arranged in a square have a pulse is only the minimum degree of numerical harmony required for a square to have magic. If there are other patterns to the numbers, the square is considered to have even greater supernatural powers. Can you discern the additional patterns in the Khajuraho square?

10-4 **ALBRECHT DÜRER'S SQUARE, 1514**

16	3	2	13
5	10	11	8
9	6	7	12
4	15	14	1

10-5 **KHAJURAHO SQUARE, TWELFTH CENTURY**

7	12	1	14
2	13	8	11
16	3	10	5
9	6	15	4

First of all, the sum of the numbers in the corners (7, 14, 9 and 4) is equal to 34, which is the pulse. Moreover, the sum of the corner numbers of *any* subsquare is also 34. For example, the numbers 13, 8, 11, 3, 10, 5, 6, 15 and 4 form a subsquare of order three, and the numbers 13, 8, 3 and 10 form a subsquare of order two; in each case the corner numbers sum to 34. How many such subsquares are there? I count thirteen.

Franklin was fond of constructing squares that had far more magic than the minimum required. In the letter to Collinson about the square in diagram 10-2, he wrote:

I then confessed to him [a Mr. Logan] that in my younger days, having once some leisure (which I still think I might have employed more usefully), I had amused myself in making these kind of magic squares, and, at length, had acquired such a knack at it, that I could fill the cells of any magic square of reasonable size with a series of numbers as fast as I could write them . . . but not being satisfied with these, which I looked on as common and easy things, I had imposed on myself more difficult tasks, and succeeded in making other magic squares with a variety of properties, and much more curious. He then showed me several in the same book [a French work] of an uncommon and more curious kind; but as I thought none of them equal to some I had remembered to have made, he desired me to let him see them; and accordingly the next time I visited him, I carried him a square which I found among my old papers, and which I will now give you with an account of its properties.

What are these properties? Franklin mentioned three. First, the sum of the four numbers in each half of any row or column comes to 130, which is half the pulse of 260. Second, the sum of the eight numbers in the "bent" diagonal (16, 63, 57, 10, 23, 40, 34 and 17) is 260, as is the sum of the eight numbers in any bent diagonal that is parallel to this one (such as 50, 8, 7, 54, 43, 26, 25 and 47). Third, the sum of the four numbers in the corners (52, 45, 16 and 17) plus the sum of the four numbers in the center (54, 43, 10 and 23) is 260.

Franklin then added a teasing remark: "So this magic square seems perfect in its kind, but these are not all its properties; there are five other curious ones which at some time I will explain to you." One of the properties he surely had in mind is the fact that the sum of the four numbers that constitute any subsquare of order two (such as 52, 61, 14 and 3, or 23, 26, 41 and 40) is 130, or half the pulse. What other properties can you deduce?

The charm of magic squares soon wore off for Franklin, and

10-6 BENJAMIN FRANKLIN'S

MAGIC CIRCLE OF CIRCLES

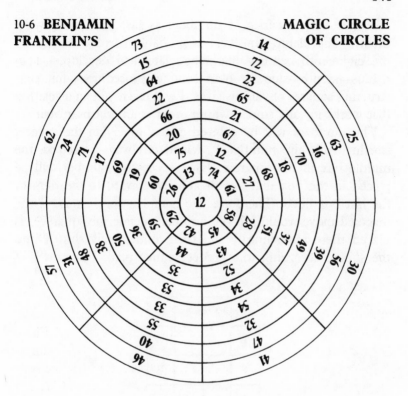

he went on to investigate the properties of other geometrical configurations of numbers. He apparently invented "the magic circle of circles," which contains all the numbers from 12 to 75 (diagram 10-6). What are its special properties? Well, the sum of the eight numbers in any ring plus the central number 12 equals 360, which is the number of degrees in a circle. Moreover, the sum of the eight numbers in any radial slice plus the central number 12 is also 360. And, most mysterious, the sum of the numbers in any four adjoining cells plus 6 (which is half the central number, 12) is 180 (half of 360).

If you floundered trying to construct a magic square of order three, you may doubt the veracity of Franklin's sweeping claim: "I could fill the cells of any magic square of reasonable size with a series of numbers as fast as I could write them." The claim, however, is probably correct because by the eighteenth century mathematicians had developed algorithms—step-by-step problem-solving procedures—for constructing squares of various sizes. I will teach you an algorithm that works for any square whose order is an odd number.

The numbers will be entered consecutively in the square, starting with the number 1, which is always placed in the middle box in the top row. Each successive number will be placed in the box that lies diagonally upward to the right of the last box filled. There are two complicating factors. If the diagonal move would put the number outside the square, it is placed there momentarily and then immediately shifted into the square according to a predetermined plan. Diagram 10-7

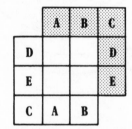

10-7

shows this plan for a square of order three: if a number is ever placed outside the square to the position of one of the shaded letters, it is immediately shifted inside the square to the position of the same letter. One need not memorize the positions of the letters, because the shift is really quite simple. In the general case of any odd-order square, a number is shifted along a straight line to the far side of the square. If the original diagonal move would put the number in a box that is already occupied, the number is placed instead in a box below its predecessor.

Diagram 10-8 shows how a square of order three is con-

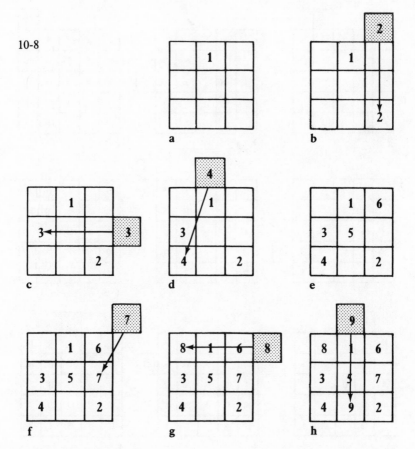

a b c d e f g h

structed according to these rules. Go through the diagram several times until the construction process becomes second nature. Then you will be ready to construct a square of order five. If you stumble, you can look at diagram 10-9, which includes an illustration each time a number must be temporarily placed outside the square.

You would make an important contribution to the theory of magic squares if you came up with a simple algorithm for constructing every addition square whose order is an even number.

Let me explain what mathematicians do know about even-

a (shaded cell: 2, above)

		1		
		2		

b (shaded cell: 4, at right of row 3)

		1		
4				
				3
		2		

c (shaded cell: 9, upper right)

		1	8	
	5	7		
4	6			
				3
			2	9

d (shaded cell: 10, at right of row 4)

		1	8	
	5	7		
4	6			
10				3
			2	9

e (shaded cell: 16, above)

		1	8	15
	5	7	14	16
4	6	13		
10	12			3
11			2	9

f (shaded cell: 17, at right of row 1)

17		1	8	15
	5	7	14	16
4	6	13		
10	12			3
11			2	9

g (shaded cell: 18, above)

17		1	8	15
	5	7	14	16
4	6	13		
10	12			3
11	18		2	9

h (shaded cell: 23, at right of row 2)

17		1	8	15
23	5	7	14	16
4	6	13	20	22
10	12	19	21	3
11	18		2	9

i (shaded cell: 25, above)

17	24	1	8	15
23	5	7	14	16
4	6	13	20	22
10	12	19	21	3
11	18	25	2	9

order squares. Efficient algorithms exist for squares whose order is a multiple of 4. Diagram 10-10 illustrates the construction of the square of order four that is similar to that in Dürer's *Melencolia I*. The first step (shown in [a]) is to put the numbers from 1 to 16 in their natural order (1, 2, 3, 4, and so on, from left to right), omitting those that fall on the principal, shaded diagonals. The next step (b) is to put the number 16 (the highest number so far omitted) in the upper left-hand cell. Now count backward from 16, cell by cell and left to right, entering a number whenever you hit a blank cell. *Voilà!* (Note in [c] that this step is equivalent to replacing each num-

	2	3	
5			8
9			12
	14	15	

16			13
	11	10	
	7	6	
4			1

16	2	3	13
5	11	10	8
9	7	6	12
4	14	15	1

	2	3			6	7	
9			12	13			16
17			20	21			24
	26	27			30	31	
	34	35			38	39	
41			44	45			48
49			52	53			56
	58	59			62	63	

64	2	3	61	60	6	7	57
9	55	54	12	13	51	50	16
17	47	46	20	21	43	42	24
40	26	27	37	36	30	31	33
32	34	35	29	28	38	39	25
41	23	22	44	45	19	18	48
49	15	14	52	53	11	10	56
8	58	59	5	4	62	63	1

that was originally omitted by its complement: the largest
number is the complement of the smallest, the second-largest
number is the complement of the second-smallest number,
and so on.)

A square of order eight (see diagram 10-11) is made by
dividing the square into four four-by-four squares, dropping
all the diagonals and then filling in the numbers in the square
as a whole by the same two-step procedure used in the order-
four case. This method works for all squares whose order is a
multiple of 4.

That leaves even-order squares that are not multiples of 4.

Mathematicians have started to work out elegant methods, but they are incomplete. Your job, should you choose to accept it and become a candidate for the mathematics hall of fame, is to pick up where the elegance peters out. Take the square of order six. The idea is to ignore for the time being the outermost cells (the blank cells in 10-12a). The remaining cells form a square of order four, which can easily be constructed by known methods. To each number in the square of order four is added the quantity $(2n - 2)$, where n is the order of the surrounding square, in this case six. You can see for yourself that the numbers in diagram 10-12a equal those in diagram 10-10c plus 10.

	26	12	13	23	
	15	21	20	18	
	19	17	16	22	
	14	24	25	11	

1	9	34	33	32	2
6	26	12	13	23	31
10	15	21	20	18	27
30	19	17	16	22	7
29	14	24	25	11	8
35	28	3	4	5	36

10-12 a   b

The trick now is to put the missing numbers (1, 2, 3, 4, 5, 6, 7, 8, 9, 10, 27, 28, 29, 30, 31, 32, 33, 34, 35 and 36) in the outermost squares. This can be accomplished by trial and error, but the problem cries out for an elegant algorithm. Let me set you on the right path. The pulse of the four-by-four square in diagram 10-12a is 74. The pulse of all squares of order six is 111 (in general, for addition squares of consecutive integers starting with 1, the pulse is $1/2n(n^2 + 1)$ where n is the order). Since 37 is the difference between 111 and 74, each pair of numbers that are added to each row, column and diagonal in diagram 10-12a must sum to 37. In other words, the numbers in each pair must be complements. The completed square is in diagram 10-12b.

The basic square of order three had much mystical significance for the early Christians. Odd numbers in general were associated with masculinity, and the ones in the square were seen to form a cross (diagram 10-13). Therefore the cross came to be regarded as the emblem of a masculine deity.

If the requirement that a square contain a series of consecutive integers is relaxed, then all sorts of spectacular hocus-pocus is possible. Diagram 10-14 depicts a multiplication square in which the product of the three numbers in each row, each column and each principal diagonal comes to 32,768, which is 2^{15}. The entries in the square can be written as in diagram 10-15, which shows that the multiplication square is just an exponential version of the addition square in diagram 10-13. The success of the multiplication square follows from an elementary truth of exponentiation:

$$2^a \times 2^b = 2^{a+b}.$$

6	1	8
7	5	3
2	9	4

10-13

64	2	256
128	32	8
4	512	16

10-14

2^6	2^1	2^8
2^7	2^5	2^3
2^2	2^9	2^4

10-15

Diagram 10-16 contains a mind-wrenching addition square of order thirteen and pulse 70,681, all of whose entries are primes (a number that can be divided evenly only by 1 and by itself). Joseph S. Madachy, in *Madachy's Mathematical Recreations*, notes that the square was "composed by a puzzlist who at the time was a prison inmate." No doubt for a long sentence! The beauty of the square is that the border can be repeatedly peeled off to leave addition squares of order eleven, order nine, order seven, order five and order three. Each peeling lowers the pulse by 10,874.

10-16

1153	8923	1093	9127	1327	9277	1063	9133	9661	1693	991	8887	8353
9967	8161	3253	2857	6823	2143	4447	8821	8713	8317	3001	3271	907
1831	8167	4093	7561	3631	3457	7573	3907	7411	3967	7333	2707	9043
9907	7687	7237	6367	4597	4723	6577	4513	4831	6451	3637	3187	967
1723	7753	2347	4603	5527	4993	5641	6073	4951	6271	8527	3121	9151
9421	2293	6763	4663	4657	9007	1861	5443	6217	6211	4111	8581	1453
2011	2683	6871	6547	5227	1873	5437	9001	5647	4327	4003	8191	8863
9403	8761	3877	4783	5851	5431	9013	1867	5023	6091	6997	2113	1471
1531	2137	7177	6673	5923	5881	5233	4801	5347	4201	3697	8737	9343
9643	2251	7027	4423	6277	6151	4297	6361	6043	4507	3847	8623	1231
1783	2311	3541	3313	7243	7417	3301	6967	3463	6907	6781	8563	9091
9787	7603	7621	8017	4051	8731	6427	2053	2161	2557	7873	2713	1087
2521	1951	9781	1747	9547	1597	9811	1741	1213	9181	9883	1987	9721

Try to arrange the prime numbers 1, 7, 13, 31, 37, 43, 61, 67 and 73 to form a magic square of order three. The answer is shown in diagram 10-17.

67	1	43
13	37	61
31	73	7

10-17

Diagram 10-18 shows an addition square that has two amusing properties. What are they? If you write each row in reverse (diagram 10-19), the resulting square is also magic! Moreover, in each case the second digit of every number can be lopped off without disturbing the magic.

15	96	93	38
94	37	16	95
36	91	98	17
97	18	35	92

10-18

83	39	69	51
59	61	73	49
71	89	19	63
29	53	81	79

10-19

I urge all of you who have a set of dominoes to arrange all twenty-eight of them so that they constitute a magic square of order seven. Treat the pips on each half of the domino as a separate number. Eight of the halves are blank. Seven should be ignored and the eighth treated as a zero, so that there are forty-nine numbers, which is precisely what is required for a seven-by-seven square. The ignored blanks should be arranged in a line along one border. The answer is shown in diagram 10-20.

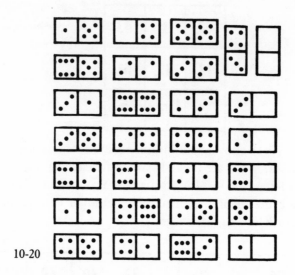

10-20

POSTMORTEM

After a version of this chapter appeared in *Science Digest,* some five hundred people sent me additional properties of Franklin's eight-by-eight square that he may have had in mind when he made his cryptic comment. Some of the properties are quite amazing.

For example, Stella Jones, of Cleveland, Ohio, pointed out that for each number in the square you can add or subtract 8 to obtain a result that will be a Knight's move in chess away from the original number! Indeed, since all the numbers are connected by Knight's moves, this might be the key to how Franklin could fill the cells of a magic square as fast as he could write them. Think of the square as being written on a piece of paper that you can roll into one of two cylinders. In one cylinder the column 52, 14, 53 . . . 16 is adjacent to the column 45, 19, 44 . . . 17; in the other the row 52, 61, 4 . . . 45 is adjacent to the row 16, 1, 64 . . . 17. Keeping these cylinders in mind, it is evident that for every number you can add 8 and subtract 8 to get results a Knight's move away. Take 16, in the bottom row, left corner. As Jones observed, 16 is a Knight's jump from 8, which is of course equal to $16 - 8$. But, given the column-to-column cylinder, 16 is also a Knight's jump from $16 + 8$, or 24.

David Lacy, of Tipton, Indiana, picked up on my observation that the sum of the four inner numbers (54, 43, 10 and 23) is 130, or $p/2$ where p is the pulse of 260. An interesting pattern emerges if one expands outward in "concentric" squares (diagram 10-21). The numbers in the second square

10-21

52	61	4	13	20	29	36	45
14	3	62	51	46	35	30	19
53	60	5	12	21	28	37	44
11	6	59	54	43	38	27	22
55	58	7	10	23	26	39	42
9	8	57	56	41	40	25	24
50	63	2	15	18	31	34	47
16	1	64	49	48	33	32	17

sum to $3p/2$. The next square provides the sum $5p/2$, and the sum of the numbers on the perimeter is $7p/2$. Adding these sums, one gets $(1 + 3 + 5 + 7)\,p/2$, or $8p$. This checks out, of course, since $1 + 2 + 3 + \ldots 64$ is $8p$.

Lacy then went on to examine octagonal arrangements of numbers in Franklin's square. He found, in diagram 10-22, that the inner octagon sums to p, the middle octagon to $2p$ and the outer octagon to $5p/2$. From this he made the discovery that any regular octagon that can be drawn on the square sums to p. (Here "regular" means that all eight sides are equal in length; thus each side consists of two numbers.) Three such octagons are shown in diagram 10-23.

It is well known that the sum of the digits in any number

10-22

that is divisible by 9 is also divisible by 9. For example, the digits in any of the numbers 81, 72 and 36, which are all divisible by 9, add up to 9. The digits in 909, which is equal to 101 × 9, sum to 18, which is of course the second multiple of 9. Indeed, the digits in 18 sum to 9. The operation of summing digits until the result is a single-digit number is called digital stimulation; 9, then, is the digital stimulation of any number that is divisible by 9. Many readers set out to determine whether or not the digital stimulation of the numbers in Franklin's square yielded a pattern. Sure enough, the digital stimulation of each row and each column is 8, which is the order of the square.

Glen McCurley, of Miami, Oklahoma, observed that the

10-23

10-24 **a**

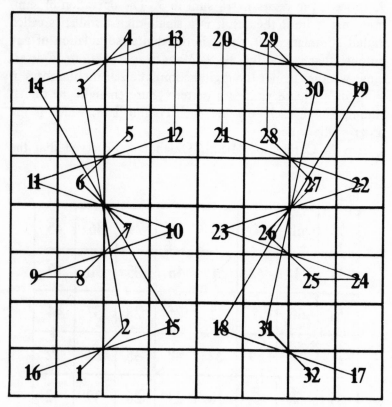

b

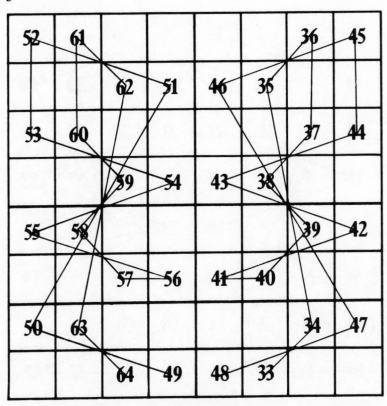

numbers in the first and seventh rows differ by 2, as do the numbers in the second and eighth rows, the third and fifth rows, and the fourth and sixth rows.

By drawing lines between consecutive numbers, David Blythe uncovered several symmetries. The orientation of 1 through 16 is identical to the orientation of 33 through 48 and is a mirror image of both the orientation of 17 through 32 and the orientation of 49 through 64 (diagram 10-24a, b). Diagram

10-25

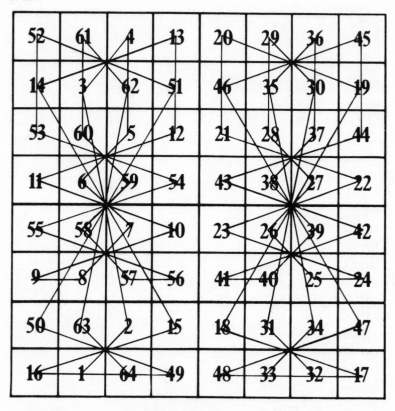

10-25 shows that the numbers have mirror symmetry about an axis between the fourth and fifth columns. It is apparent, further, that each horizontal half of the square also exhibits mirror symmetry about a horizontal axis.

Connecting the numbers in this way is a good way to expose underlying symmetries, and I urge you to do this for the other squares we've looked at.

11

The Tower of Bramah:
How Long Until Doomsday?

Rubik's Cube is not the only mechanical puzzle to have taken the world by storm. About one hundred years ago an ancient Oriental puzzle called the Tower of Bramah (or the Tower of Hanoi) made its debut in the West and immediately became all the rage.

The Tower of Bramah, which is still popular today, consists of three vertical pegs mounted on a horizontal board (diagram 11-1). Any number of wooden disks, usually eight, that differ in diameter are threaded onto one of the pegs, so that they form a conical tower, the disks decreasing in diameter from bottom to top. The object of the puzzle is to shift the tower to another peg in the fewest number of moves. A move is the transfer of a disk from one peg to another. There is a catch, however, as there always is: a disk can never be placed on top of a smaller disk.

You don't have to go out and buy the Tower of Bramah in order to try it. You won't be guilty of patent infringement if you cut disks out of cardboard and simply stack them. Or, if you're a klutz like me, you can create the same puzzle by using eight index cards that are numbered from 1 to 8. The

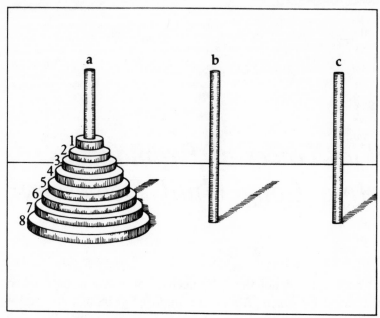

11-1

idea here is that you cannot play a card on top of one with a smaller number.

The puzzle is associated with a wonderful legend, which W. W. Rouse Ball describes in his 1892 encyclopedia of puzzles, *Mathematical Recreations and Essays:*

> In the great temple at Benares, beneath the dome which marks the center of the world, rests a brass plate in which are fixed three diamond needles, each a cubit high and as thick as the body of a bee. On one of these needles at the Creation, God placed sixty-four disks of pure gold, the largest disk resting on the brass plate, and the others getting smaller and smaller up to the top one. This is the Tower of Bramah. Day and night unceasingly the priests transfer the disks from one diamond needle to another according

to the fixed and immutable laws of Bramah, which require that the priest on duty not move more than one disk at a time and that he must place the disk on a needle so that there is no smaller disk below it. When the sixty-four disks shall have been thus transferred from the needle on which at the Creation God placed them to one of the other needles, tower, temple, and Brahmins alike will crumble into dust, and with a thunderclap the world will vanish.

Before you read beyond this paragraph, I implore you to figure out how many moves the priests will have to make in order to complete the transfer. Moreover, if the legend is true, how long do we have until doomsday?

Futility was in store for anyone who tackled this problem by physically manipulating sixty-four disks or sixty-four cards. Empirical methods will take you only so far; the Tower of Bramah must be cracked by abstract reasoning. The first thing to do is introduce a notation for expressing the moves. Think of the disks as numbered from 1 to 64 in order of increasing diameter, and the pegs as labeled *a*, *b*, and *c*. The tower is initially on *a*. The transfer of the smallest disk (*1*) from *a* to *b* would be designated *1b*.

The key to solving the problem is to look empirically at simple cases (that is, at towers consisting of only a few disks) and then to generalize to the case of sixty-four disks. A mathematician would begin with the simplest case, a "tower" one disk high. It takes only one move, of course, to transfer the tower to another peg. Consider a tower of two disks. The solution takes three moves: *1b, 2c, 1c*. The case of three disks is a bit more complex; seven moves are required: *1b, 2c, 1c, 3b, 1a, 2b, 1b*. The case of four disks has a fifteen-move solution: *1b, 2c, 1c, 3b, 1a, 2b, 1b, 4c, 1c, 2a, 1a, 3c, 1b, 2c, 1c*.

The number of moves increases rapidly as the number of

disks is increased. Luckily, we already have enough information from which to extrapolate to the general case of n disks. The following table summarizes what we know:

Disks	Moves
1	1
2	3
3	7
4	15

The next step is to find a pattern to the numbers in the table. The moves are growing exponentially. Indeed, the number of moves required is equal to $2^n - 1$, where n is the number of disks. If you need convincing, try checking the formula in the case of five disks. The formula $2^n - 1$ yields 31, which is what it should take when you do the problem empirically.

Mathematicians avoid the empirical as often as possible. A mathematician would solve the Tower of Bramah by looking at only one empirical case, the trivial case of a single disk. The reasoning is as follows. Suppose we know that the solution for n disks takes x moves. On the basis of this knowledge, can we determine how many moves it would take for $n + 1$ disks? Yes, we can. We know it takes x moves to transfer n of the $n + 1$ disks to another peg. It then takes one move to shift the $(n + 1)$th disk to the free peg. Then, to move the tower of n disks onto the $(n + 1)$th disk requires x moves because it is identical to the problem of shifting a tower of n disks from one peg to another. Thus, a total of $2x + 1$ moves is required for transferring $n + 1$ disks.

So far the mathematician has reasoned abstractly. Now he turns briefly to the empirical. He sees that in the case of $n = 1$, one move is required. Having examined only one empirical solution, he can generalize to all n. In each case, x is the number of moves in the previous computation (the $n - 1$

case). For $n = 2$ he uses the formula $2x + 1$, where x is 1 (the number of moves in the case $n = 1$). Thus, $2x + 1$ yields 3. For $n = 3$, the formula $2x + 1$, where $x = 3$, yields 7. And for $n = 4$, the formula $2x + 1$, where $x = 7$, yields 15. The mathematician's results agree with our empirical findings. The mathematician would naturally spot the same $2^n - 1$ pattern that we found.

That brings us back to the sixty-four-disk Tower of Bramah. The number of moves needed to transfer the tower is $2^{64} - 1$, or 18,446,744,073,709,551,615. How soon might the transfer be effected? God works awfully fast (if we may judge from the six days it took Him to create the world), and so it is reasonable to assume that His ombudsmen on earth are also swift. If the priests move disks at the incredibly fast rate of one per second, it will take them nearly 600 billion years to shift the tower to another needle. That makes this doomsday scenario as likely as Immanuel Velikovsky's.

Astrophysicists think that the universe is at most 20 billion years old. In mathematics, a special status is accorded computational principles that are solvable in principle, but only by a computer the size of the universe operating for at least as long as the age of the universe! The status is one of being "intrinsically difficult"—a delightfully euphemistic way of saying that the problems defy computer analysis. Larry Stockmeyer of IBM argued in *Scientific American* that the most powerful computer conceivable "could not be larger than the known universe (less than 100 billion light-years in diameter), could not consist of hardware smaller than the proton (10^{-13} centimeter in diameter) and could not transmit information faster than the speed of light (3×10^8 meters per second). Given these limitations, such a computer could consist of at most 10^{126} pieces of hardware." Intrinsically difficult problems are those computational problems that, although they are known to be solvable, would stump this ideal computer for at least 20 billion years. The problem of writing down the moves necessary to transfer the sixty-four-disk Tower of Bramah turns out to be an intrinsically difficult problem.

From playing with the Tower of Bramah, you may have discovered the patterns inherent in the solution. For example, every other move involves the smallest disk. Another pattern is apparent if the pegs are thought of as being arranged not in a line but in a circle. In that case, all odd-numbered disks are moved in the same direction—say, clockwise—whereas all even-numbered disks are moved in the opposite direction—counterclockwise. With these patterns in mind, it is easy to make the moves at top speed, if you want to show off your mastery of the puzzle.

12

A Xenophobe Luddite from Mounts, or the Rise of the Scientific Limerick

I sat next to the Duchess at tea.
It was just as I feared it would be:
Her rumblings abdominal
Were truly phenomenal,
And everyone thought it was me!
   —*Woodrow Wilson*

There was a young girl of Shanghai
Who was so exceedingly shy,
That undressing at night,
She turned out the light
For fear of the All-seeing eye.
   —*Bertrand Russell*

The writing of limericks by a U.S. President and a Nobel laureate has lent respectability to a form of verse that was once devoted to the entertainment of infants but has now become an outlet for cynical, unprintable musings on infanticide, algolagnia, vivisection and a host of other disturbing subjects. To a lesser extent, the limerick has always served as a noble vehicle for sardonic commentary on intellectual issues, particularly matters metaphysical and scientific. The couplet in Wilson's verse, for example, can be appropriated for a limerick about Luddites, the antitechnology rioters in England who smashed textile machinery in the 1810s:

A xenophobe Luddite from Mounts
Ate abaci up by the ounce.
His rumblings abdominal
Were truly phenomenal
'Cause it's what inside that counts.

Other limericks have addressed the subject of counting in a less oblique way. Witness one of the first limericks to appear in print, in *Ye Book of Sense: A Companion to the Book of Nonsense*, published in Philadelphia in the middle of the nineteenth century:

There was an old man who said—"Do
Tell me how I'm to add two and two!
I'm not very sure
That it does not make four;
But I fear that is almost too few."

As arithmetic computations became more complex, so did the limericks:

A formidable student at Trinity
Solved the square root of infinity.
It gave him such fidgets
To count up the digits
He chucked math and took up divinity.

Limericks have also kept up with developments in such abstract branches of mathematics as topology. The properties of the Möbius strip (a one-sided band that can be cut in half lengthwise without falling apart) have been delightfully captured:

A mathematician confided
A Möbius strip is one-sided.
You'll get quite a laugh
If you cut one in half
For it stays in one piece when divided.

Also immortalized in verse is the topological object known as the Klein bottle (a peculiar one-sided bottle formed from two Möbius strips):

A mathematician named Klein
Thought the Möbius strip was divine.
Said he, "If you glue
The edges of two,
You'll get a weird bottle like mine."

In a few inspired cases, mathematics has been coupled with the traditional concern of limericks: sex.

A mathematician named Hall
Has a hexahedronical ball,
And the cube of its weight
Times his pecker, plus eight,
Is his phone number—give him a call.

Why are limericks so popular? Well, it's partly the shape of the thing that gives the old limerick ring. Plus more than a bit of off-color wit, and a tag line that ends with a zing.

Moreover, aside from psychoanalysis, the limerick is one of

the few institutionalized ways of expressing our most childish thoughts on sex.

There was a young man from Racine
Who invented a fucking machine:
Both concave and convex,
It would fit either sex,
With attachments for those in between.

There was a young fellow named Chris
Whose sex life was strangely amiss.
For even with Venus
His recalcitrant penis
Would seldom do better than t
                        h
                        i
                        s.

More limericks seem to have been written in 1907 and 1908 than in all other years combined. The English periodical *London Opinion* inspired the poetic frenzy with a series of contests in which readers could win £50 by writing witty tag lines for unfinished limericks. The entrance fee of a six-penny postal order did nothing to discourage participation; on the contrary, it almost brought down the postal service. An official told the House of Commons that in the second half of 1907 the public "would have bought, in the ordinary way, between 700,000 and 800,000 six-penny postal orders. They actually bought no less than 11,400,000—fourteen times as many!" In the most successful contest, 700,000 Britons submitted tag lines for the following incomplete limerick:

There was a young lady of Ryde
Whose locks were consid'rably dyed.
The hue of her hair
Made everyone stare . . .

The winning entry was:

"She's piebald, she'll die bald!" they cried.

Many other English-language periodicals in Europe moved quickly to cash in on the limerick craze by holding contests of their own. The notable exception was the *Limerick* (Ireland) *Times*, whose editor said: "I am sick unto death of obscure English towns that exist seemingly for the sole accommodation of these so-called limerick writers—and even sicker of their residents, all of whom suffer from physical deformities and spend their time dismembering relatives at fancy dress balls."

How, you may wonder, did the limerick come to have the name of an Irish town (and county)? Scholarly opinion is divided, although historians of nonsense verse agree that the word *limerick* was coined in the 1890s. Some authorities trace the name to a whimsical Irish folk song with the catchy chorus "Won't you come up to Limerick?" Other scholars point to the (unfortunately undocumented) practice of soldiers from Limerick who, on returning from battle in the 1750s, burst into limericklike song; one is reminded of raunchy college fighting cheers such as "The freshmen down at Yale get no tail." Still others think that the name is based on nothing more than the perception of Ireland as a poetic land.

In any event, it was an Englishman, Edward Lear, who made the limerick a popular form of verse. Born in London in 1812, the youngest of twenty-one children, Lear was an illustrator who specialized in anatomically accurate renderings of animals, particularly birds. By the age of fifteen he was earning a tidy sum drawing nature studies for hospital corridors and doctors' offices. When he was twenty he published his first book, *The Family of the Psittacidae*, which was a collection of color plates of parrots. In 1834 the Earl of Derby commissioned Lear to make an album of his private menagerie. Lear gladly consented and put in overtime amusing the

Earl's grandchildren with limericks he composed.

In 1846 the limericks, along with Lear's wacky line drawings, were published in *The Book of Nonsense*. When the book was reissued in the 1870s it was a huge success, and the splendid new form of nonsense verse spread through Europe. During Lear's lifetime—he died in 1888—the word *limerick* was never used; the 212 that he wrote were called *learics* by his contemporaries. In his declining years Lear lamented that he would be remembered not for his precise renderings of birds but for his popularization of the limerick and for his poem "The Owl and the Pussy-Cat."

If it were not for the humorous illustrations in *The Book of Nonsense*, the limerick might have died there. Most of Lear's limericks were dull because the last line merely repeated the rhyme word of the first line—and often much of the rest of the line as well.

There was an Old Man with a beard,
Who sat on a horse when he reared;
But they said, "Never mind!"
You will fall off behind,
You propitious Old Man with a beard!"

There was a Young Lady of Ryde,
Whose shoe-strings were seldom untied;
She purchased some clogs,
And some small spotty dogs,
And frequently walked about Ryde.

There was a Young Lady whose bonnet,
Came untied when the birds sate upon it;
But she said, "I don't care!
All the birds in the air
Are welcome to sit on my bonnet!"

The limerick survived because the next generation of composers did away with the lazy last line. Indeed, the tag line, ending on a fresh rhyme word, delivers the punch. A good limerick builds until it explodes in frenzied wit in the last line. Three famous examples:

There was a young lady of Niger
Who smiled as she rode on a tiger.
They returned from the ride
With the lady inside
And the smile on the face of the tiger.

A wonderful bird is the pelican
His mouth can hold more than his belican.
He can take in his beak
Enough food for a week.
I'm darned if I know how the helican.

An epicure dining at Crewe
Found quite a large mouse in his stew
Said the waiter, "Don't shout
And wave it about,
Or the rest will be wanting one too."

The tag line is so critical in the modern limerick that, in itself, it has become the subject of limericks:

There was a young fellow named Greer
Who hadn't an atom of fear.
He indulged a desire
To touch a live wire—
Most any last line will do here.

There was a young man of Japan
Whose limericks never would scan.
When someone asked why

He replied with a sigh,
"It's because I always try to get as many words into the last line as
    I possibly can."

Another young poet in China
Had a feeling for rhythm much fina.
His limericks tend
To come to an end
Quite suddenly.

The motif established in the last limerick has been carried
further:

There was a young man from Crewe
Whose limericks would end at line two.

And further:

There was a young man from Verdun.

And even further:

The enigmatologist Martin Gardner sees the Verdun verse as
the limerick equivalent of the liar's paradox (the self-contra-
dictory statement, "I am lying"). To complete it in your mind
("Whose limericks would end at line one") is to violate its
spirit; nonetheless, if it is not completed, it is meaningless.
    In the 1890s it was customary to parody Lear's innocuous
style. For Lear's

There was a Young Lady of Norway
Who casually sat in a doorway.
When the door squeezed her flat,

She exclaimed, "What of that?"
This courageous Young Lady of Norway,

an anonymous wit substituted:

There was a Young Lady of Norway
Who hung by her toes in a doorway.
She said to her beau:
"Just look at me, Joe,
I think I've discovered one more way."

The best parody is of the following verse:

There was an Old Man in a tree
Who was horribly bored by a bee.
When they said, "Does it buzz?"
He replied, "Yes, it does!
It's a regular brute of a bee."

Sir William Schwenk Gilbert wrote:

There was an Old Man of St. Bees
Who was stung in the arm by a Wasp.
When asked, "Does it hurt?"
He replied, "No, it doesn't;
I'm so glad it wasn't a hornet."

Lear, however, deserves more credit than he normally gets.
The first line of his limericks often gives geographical information ("There was a Young Man of Dundee"), a practice that
has been followed to this day. Moreover, a few of his limericks
are inspired, even if they do repeat rhyme words or force
words to rhyme through weird pronounciations. For example:

There was a Young Man who said, "Hush!
I perceive a young bird in that bush!"

When they said, "Is it small?"
He replied, "Not at all!
It's five times the size of the bush!"

In Lear's verses one can even find shades of the preoccupation of twentieth-century limericks with the macabre and the perverse:

There was an Old Man on some rocks
Who shut up his wife in a box.
When she said, "Let me out!"
He exclaimed, "Without doubt!
You will pass all your life in that box."

There was an Old Man on a hill
Who seldom, if ever, stood still;
He ran up and down,
In his Grandmother's gown,
Which adorned that Old Man on a hill.

Lear's limericks were sufficiently inoffensive, however, that Queen Victoria herself had no second thoughts about hiring him to teach her how to draw.

Besides adding a snappy tag line, the second generation of limerick writers improved on Lear by turning to tongue-twisting wordplay and uncommon rhymes. Consider:

When a jolly young fisher named Fisher
Went fishing for fish in a fissure.
A fish with a grin,
Pulled the fisherman in.
Now they're fishing the fissure for Fisher.

There once was a sculptor named Phidias
Whose statues, by some, were thought hideous.

He made Aphrodite
Without even a nightie,
Which shocked all the fussy fastidious.

Verbal high jinks, however, go only so far. The next phase
in the evolution of the modern limerick was a move away from
tame subject matter. As Don Marquis put it, "There are three
kinds of limerick: limericks to be told when ladies are present,
limericks to be told when ladies are absent, but clergymen are
present—and limericks." George Bernard Shaw was disap-
pointed that the last kind had to be left to oral tradition. Shaw
hoped that eventually "sufficient limericks which shall be de-
cent as well as witty and ingenious may accumulate and be
collected in a volume that a reputable publisher dares touch."

Shaw's hope came true in the form of the rise of the metaphysical and scientific limerick, of which an early example by
Oliver Wendell Holmes, Sr., is still among the best:

God's plan made a hopeful beginning
But man spoiled his chances by sinning.
We trust that the story
Will end in God's glory
But, at present, the other side's winning.

The counterintuitive aspects of the theory of relativity provided much material for limericks. The first two quoted below
are the work of A. H. Reginald Buller, an expert on mush-
rooms. The authors of the other two are not known.

There was a young lady named Bright,
Whose speed was far faster than light.
She went out one day
In a relative way
And returned the previous night.

To her friends said the Bright one in chatter,
"I have learned something new about matter:
As my speed was so great
Much increased was my weight
Yet I failed to become any fatter!"

There was a young fellow named Fisk
Whose fencing was agile and brisk.
So fast was his action,
The Fitzgerald contraction
Diminished his sword to a disk.

A wonderful family is Stein
There's Gert and there's Ep and there's Ein
Gert's verses are punk
Ep's statues are junk
And nobody understands Ein.

In a paper on anthropic cosmology (the theory, now in
vogue, that the universe would not exist if there were no humans to observe it) the physicist John Wheeler cites limericks
that are a trumped-up version of the old tree-falls-in-the-forest
paradox:

There was a young man who said, "God,
It always has struck me as odd
That the sycamore tree
Simply ceases to be
When there's no one about in the quad."

"Dear Sir, Your astonishment's odd;
I am always about in the quad:
And that's why the tree
Will continue to be,
Since observed by, Yours faithfully, God."

Wheeler takes issue with His answer and offers instead the incredible view that it's the mere presence of human observers at any point in the history of the universe, regardless of whether or not anyone ever sees the tree, that ensures that the sycamore continues to be.

On a lighter note, limericks have recorded the behavior of organisms, both macroscopic and microscopic:

The thoughts of the rabbit on sex
Are seldom, if ever, complex.
For a rabbit in need
Is a rabbit indeed,
And does just as a person suspects.

An amoeba named Sam and his brother
Were having a drink with each other.
In the midst of their quaffing
They split their sides laughing.
And each of them now is a mother.

As might be expected, a whole slew of limericks poke fun at Freud. Most are not fit for ladies or clergy, but neither, for that matter, is Freud.

The youths who frequent picture palaces
Have no use for psychoanalysis
And though Dr. Freud
Is distinctly annoyed
They cling to their long-standing fallacies.

Recently a robot manufacturer offered to put up one of its helpmates if I would somehow give it away in my puzzle column in *Science Digest*. Given the colorful tradition of scientific limericks, I decided to hold a contest for the limerick that best described the emerging relation between robots and human beings. The prize, of course, was the two-thousand-dollar home robot, which serves alcoholic beverages and attends to other necessary household functions.

More than five thousand readers responded to my call for limericks about robots, and Lora and I had a tough time picking the best one. In another limerick contest, the judges chose the winner from hundreds of entries by putting aside the bawdy submissions and rewarding the sole nursery-clean one. I was concerned that we recognize real talent and not someone who merely happened to stumble on a clever limerick. As Sir Arthur Eddington once said, in a similar context,

> There once was a breathy baboon
> Who always breathed down a bassoon,
> For he said, "It appears
> That in billions of years
> I shall certainly hit on a tune."

My fears were eased by William R. Bennett, Jr., of Yale University, who computed the odds that the plays of Shakespeare could have been written not by Francis Bacon but by chimpanzees. Bennett's conclusion is quoted in *The Literary Life and Other Curiosities:* "If a trillion monkeys were to type ten randomly chosen characters a second it would take, on the average, more than a trillion times as long as the universe has been in existence just to produce the sentence 'To be or not to be, that is the question.' "

I was also worried that in probing the relation between humans and robots, we might come across as fools by writing limericks that the robots themselves could have produced. I could find no examples in the literature of robot-written limericks, but the computer poetry I did find convinced me that in this domain machines pose no challenge. For example, a high-school student in Florida programmed an IBM 709 computer to arrange seventy-seven phrases in poetic quatrains. It spewed out:

Darkly the peaceful trees clashed
In the serene sun
While the heart heard
The swift moon stopped silently.

Cybernetic haiku is scarcely any better:

Pine in the sun
A sparkling firefly in the hill
Falling river.

A spring meadow . . .
The moon sleeps under a bush
Broken blue snowflake.

All white in the buds
I flash snowpeaks in the spring.
Bang the sun has fogged.

And now . . . what you've been waiting for . . . the announcement of the winner of the home robot! I was proud to give the contraption to Gloria Maxson of Whittier, California. Her avocation is—get ready for this—writing robot limericks. She sent me seventy-two witty ones, a few of which appeared in *National Review* and *Creative Computing*. And I thought *I* did weird things to make money! From time to time, Maxson has earned a living in more conventional ways, such as giving guitar lessons. Here are seven of her best limericks:

Said a robot who never pulls punches,
"It is one of my gloomier hunches
I descended from brutes
In Brooks Brothers suits,
Who watered at martini lunches."

A robotical tenor named Scotti
About singing love songs was dotty.
But he hadn't the glands
That such singing demands,
So he sang with a choir of castrati.

A robot who reckons up rows
Of numbers with infinite 0's
Regards Charles Babbage
As just an old cabbage
Who counted on fingers and toes.

A robot took pleasure immense
In programmings of sexual sense.
And beholding a pail
He thought was female,
Cried out, "Vive la différence!"

A robot with lofty inflection
Read Stein in the poetry section,
But read it "Arose
Is arose is arose"
And thought it concerned resurrection.

The robotic geneticist squirms
When asked what eugenics affirms,
And will not orate
On man's future fate
In sacred or secular terms.

The robotical judge never knew
Which ethical dictum was true:
"To forgive is divine"
Or "Vengeance is mine."
So he simply rotated the two.

The runners-up in the contest are also clever:

A remarkable robot named Sally
Was created in Silicon Valley.
In her microchip heart,
She was programmed for art.
Now this dolly's a dilly like Dali!
                    —Robert Turner

To say that my robot's desire
Is nothing but circuits and wire
Is just the conceit
Of a head and two feet
Packaged in fleshly attire.
                    —Stephen J. Mauritz

On the day two robots were wed
The preacher leaned over and said,
"I know you'll compute,
But you cannot refute
That children are just in your head."
                    —James C. Miller

Jimmy Connors said, "I'm going to beatcha,"
To the strange-looking, chrome-plated creature.
But it whipped him that set,
And quipped at the net,
"Bjorn Cyborg's the name. Glad to meetcha."
                    —Tom Sales

POSTMORTEM

A fellow paradoxologist, who pleaded for anonymity, told me
that he fights insomnia not by counting sheep but by compos-
ing limericks that are capsule biographies of scientific luminar-
ies. One sleepless night he came up with these gems:

A bellicose feller named Teller
That prominent arms race impeller
Promotes with aplomb
The hydrogen bomb
And tells the uncertain they're yeller.

A Greek who was really quite clever
Proposed a fantastic endeavor.
He claimed if he found
A firm piece of ground
He could move the world with a lever.

It is curious that a scientific figure was the subject of the
first clerihew, a form of biographical nonsense verse that is
popular in England. One morning in 1891 the sixteen-year-old
preppie Edmund Clerihew Bentley, seated at his study in St.
Paul's School, London, was endeavoring to master "those
measures which Julius Caesar had found, to his regret, to be
unavoidable in dealing with the Usipetes and the Tencteri."
Bentley glanced in his notebook and was astonished to find
that he had unknowingly penned four dotty lines:

Sir Humphrey Davy
Detested gravy,
He lived in the odium
Of having discovered sodium.

Such was the first representative of the new form of verse that
would come to be called by Bentley's middle name.

The clerihew has even less structure than the limerick, and
so it is ideally suited to neophyte poets who have no patience
with meter. The requirements of the clerihew are few and can
be freely ignored. The clerihew has four short lines, the first
of which is the name of the personality whose essence is being
captured. The rhyme scheme is *aabb*, and the intent is wacki-
ness as well as biographical accuracy. (In regard to the latter,

it should be noted that when Bentley "discovered" the first clerihew, he felt compelled to append an apology: "This widely-diffused and abundant element [sodium] was, in a sense, discovered in 1736 by Duhamel, he first recognized it as a distinct substance; but it was first obtained in the metallic state by Davy in 1807.")

The clerihew caught on immediately at St. Paul's School and, soon, somehow found its way into, in Bentley's words, "the hands of connoisseurs of idiocy everywhere." Before you put pen to paper, consider the following examples of Bentley's clerihumor:

Sir Christopher Wren
Said, "I'm going to dine with some men.
If anybody calls
Say I'm designing St. Paul's."

George the Third
Ought never to have occurred
One can only wonder
At so grotesque a blunder.

Louis XI
Was contemporary with Henry VII.
I am very glad he
Was not contemporary with me.

"I quite realized," said Columbus,
"That the Earth was not a rhombus,
But I *am* a little annoyed
To find it an oblate spheroid."

It was a weakness of Voltaire's
To forget to say his prayers,
And one which to his shame
He never overcame.

14

A Horse Divided
and Other More or Less
Ancient Conundrums

One of my favorite puzzles is an ancient Arab chestnut based on a man's will. The man left his three sons 17 camels. To the eldest he promised half, to the middle child he promised a third and to the youngest he promised a ninth. Try as they might, the children could not figure out how to divide up the camels, and so they consulted a wise man, who they thought knew about camels because he was riding one.

The wise man was very sagacious. He turned to the three boys and said: "I know the will only gives you 17 camels. But I am a generous man. I will add my own camel to the lot, bringing the total to 18." The boys wondered how the wise man would get home, but they thanked him profusely by bowing left and right.

He turned to the oldest child. "The will stipulates that you shall receive half the camels. One half of 18 is 9."

To the middle child he said: "The will states that you shall receive one third of the camels. One third of 18 is 6."

And to the youngest he said: "The will stipulates that you

shall receive one ninth the camels. One ninth of 18 is 2."

The boys were elated because they had received more than the will called for. The wise man was happy that they were happy, jumped on his camel and galloped away.

"Wait a moment!" the youngest cried. "He's hoodwinked us. He said that he was giving up his camel. Now he's riding it away!"

The eldest, and the wisest, of the three calmed his siblings down. "Don't be so rash to pass judgment. Thanks to his sage counsel, we're still better off. Under the will I was entitled to 17/2 camels. I actually received 9 camels. Nine minus 17/2 is 1/2. I got 1/2 a camel more than Father willed. You, peewee, you have 2 camels. The will provides you with only 17/9 camels. You made out like a bandit with 1/9 of a camel extra. And you, middle brother, you have 6 camels, which is 1/3 more than the 17/3 camels willed you."

And yet, in spite of the boys' good fortune, they collectively had 17 camels (9 + 6 + 2)—exactly what their father had left them. How is that possible?

Everything adds up, so to speak, if the figures are kept straight. Although the father's estate consists of 17 camels, the instructions in the will do not result in all the camels being passed on to the sons. The fractions mentioned in the will—17/9, 17/3 and 17/2—come to only 16 1/18 (because 17/9 + 17/3 + 17/2 = 34/18 + 102/18 + 153/18 = 289/18 = 16 1/18). The gift "horse" the boys received—1/9, 1/3 and 1/2—comes to 17/18 of a camel (because 1/9 + 1/3 + 1/2 = 2/18 + 6/18 + 9/18 = 17/18). Sure enough, the 16 1/18 willed camels plus the 17/18 extra camel equals 17 camels. The wise man rides off on the eighteenth camel. Thus, all are accounted for.

Mind benders that involve extra or missing objects are common in the history of paradoxology. Dozens of people have asked me to explain the answer to the following familiar teaser: Three weary travelers arrive at a motel. They are lucky because there's only one room left, for which the night manager charges them $30. They each pay $10. When the day manager comes on duty, he examines the books and finds that the three men should have paid only $25. He sends the bellhop to their room to give them a refund of $5. Not knowing how to divide $5 evenly among three men, he gives them back only $3 and pockets the other $2. Naturally, the three men each take $1.

Each man, then, has paid $9, the room costing them a total of $27. The bellhop kept $2. That makes $29 accounted for. What happened to the missing $1?

A dollar is not really missing. Of the original $30, the manager has $25, the men have $3 and the bellboy has $2.

All sorts of weird results are possible if one adds apples and oranges. Suppose, in the previous problem, the day manager finds that the room costs $20. He sends the bellboy to the room to refund the $10. Again, the bellboy doesn't know how to divide $10 three ways. He's upset with the manager, so he gives the men only $3 and pockets the other $7. And now for some arithmetic sleight of mind: the men paid a total of $27. Add to this sum the $7 the bellboy filched and you have $34. Four dollars have emerged from nowhere! The absurdity of this result should convince you to be careful what you add to what.

Another modern twist on the ancient Arab twister has three boy going on a picnic. The youngest brings five dishes, the eldest brings three dishes, and the other, who hates to cook, throws $8 into the pot. Suppose all the dishes are of equal value and that $8 was the proper amount to contribute. How should the money be divided between the boys who brought the food?

Since $8 is the just contribution of each picnicker, the meal is worth three times $8, or $24. There are eight dishes, and so each one is worth $3 ($24 divided by 8). The youngest brought $15 worth of food, which is $7 too much. And the eldest brought $9 worth of food, which is $1 too much. Therefore, of the $8, the youngest gets $7 and the eldest $1.

I now want to present four cerebrum benders that have come to my attention recently. The answers appear at the end of the chapter.

COFFEE BREAK: Brilliant scientists are notoriously absent-minded. David Hilbert, perhaps the greatest German mathematician of all time, was hosting a party at his home. His wife noticed that his tie was stained and suggested that he go upstairs and change it. He gladly complied. After considerable time had passed and Hilbert had not returned, his wife went to fetch him. She found him sleeping, undressed, in the bedroom. When she woke him, he explained that he had disrobed because he always did that after taking off his tie.

Speaking of brilliant scientists, another mathematician, who shall remain nameless, tied a coffee cup to his wrist each night before he went to bed because he was afraid that he might forget to have his coffee in the morning. He always took a loop of string, threaded it through the handle of the cup and tied the free end snugly to his wrist (as shown in diagram 14-1). Once when he woke up he had forgotten whether he had to cut the string or slip it off his wrist in order to dislodge the cup. Can you help him out? Try this first in your mind's eye.

14-1

A NOT SO DUMB QUESTION: All of us know of sentences that are more easily written than spoken. A familiar example is the tongue twister, such as "Peter Piper picked a peck of pickled peppers." Likewise, there are sentences that are easier to say than to write. This is the case when the sentence is loaded with common words that have tricky spellings. I challenge you to go one step further and devise a sentence that can be effortlessly uttered but is *impossible* to write. Perhaps you're already wondering how I'm going to communicate the answer!

ALL BOTTLED UP: The sight of a miniature ship in a bottle is spellbinding no matter how many you've seen before. You know it's not an illusion because it's right before your eyes and the bottle is seamless. Yet the ship is too large for it to have been forced down the bottleneck. What's the secret? The hull is assembled outside the bottle and the masts, the sails and the rigging, to which little strings have been attached, are laid flat on the hull. The collapsed ship is then pushed into the bottle. When the strings are gently pulled, the ship springs to life like a marionette, as the masts, sails and rigging are hoisted into place.

All this sounds fine, but in practice it's another matter. The nimblest of fingers are required. The klutzes among us need not despair, however, because they can create a comparable mystery: a whole, peeled, hard-boiled egg in a soda-pop bottle whose opening is considerably smaller than the egg. How does the egg get bottled up?

GARBLED GREETINGS: Perhaps it's just my friends and not a national trend, but each year the greeting cards I receive get progressively stranger, as bathos gives way to wit. An anonymous well-wisher, who must have known of my interest in astronomy, sent me a card that depicts exuberant extraterrestrials jumping around on the surface of a multicolored orb. The caption reads: "Greetings from Uranus."

Another card was blank except for the enigmatic inscription "ABCDEFGHIJKMNOPQRSTUVWXYZ." What does it mean?

ANSWERS

COFFEE BREAK: The cup can be freed simply by grabbing the single strand at a point where it crosses the doubled-up part, pulling on that point until a large loop is formed, then slipping the loop down over the top of the cup. Try it if you're skeptical.

NOT SO DUMB QUESTION: The answer is something a school-marm might say: "There are three ways to write the word _____: 'their,' 'there' and 'they're.' " You have no problem filling the blank when you utter the sentence, but how can you possibly do it when you try to write it down?

ALL BOTTLED UP: Stand the bottle upright in a pot of boiling water. (Make sure no water flows into the bottle.) When the bottle has heated, gently set the egg in the opening. Take the pot off the stove and the bottle out of the pot. The air in the bottle, which expanded because of the heating, will now contract, creating a partial vacuum that will draw the egg inside. Try it if you don't believe it.

GARBLED GREETINGS: The inscription means "No L"—that is, "Noel."

Further Reading

Long Words

Mrs. Byrne's Dictionary of Unusual, Obscure and Preposterous Words. Josefa Heifetz Byrne. Citadel Press, 1974.

Triskaidekaphobia

"Thirteen at Table." Vincent Starrett. *Gourmet,* November 1966.
Dr. Crypton and His Problems. Dr. Crypton. St. Martin's Press, 1982.

The SAT Snafu

"Youth Outwits Merit Exam, Raising 240,000 Scores." *The New York Times,* March 17, 1981.
"A Second Student Wins Challenge on Answer to Math Exam Problem." *The New York Times,* March 24, 1981.
"Pyramids of Test Question 44 Opens a Pandora's Box." *The New York Times,* April 14, 1981.
"Math Error Fouls SAT Test Scores." *Chicago Sun-Times,* May 25, 1982.

Science Humor

The Journal of Irreproducible Results. Dr. George H. Scherr, editor. Workman Publishing, 1983.

Anagrams

Language on Vacation: An Olio of Orthographical Oddities. Dimitri A.
Borgmann. Charles Scribner's Sons, 1965.
Palindromes and Anagrams. Howard W. Bergerson, Dover Publications, 1973.

Weird Coincidences

The Roots of Coincidence. Arthur Koestler. Vintage Books, 1972.

Acrostics

Oddities and Curiosities of Words and Literature. C. C. Bombaugh.
Dover Publications, 1961.
The Humorous Verses of Lewis Carroll. Dover Publications, 1960.

The Shakespeare-Authorship Controversy

The Shakespearean Ciphers Examined. William F. Friedman and
Elizabeth S. Friedman. Cambridge University Press, 1957.
The Poacher from Stratford. Frank W. Wadsworth. University of
California Press, 1958.
"Honorificabilitudinitatibus." E.L. *Baconiana,* Vol. 1 New Series,
November 1893, pages 170–171.
"Honorificabilitudinitatibus." George Stronach. *Baconiana,* Vol. 3
Third Series, July 1905, pages 185–186.

Chess in Fiction

The Defense. Vladimir Nabokov. Capricorn Books, 1964.
The Annotated Alice. Lewis Carroll, with annotations by Martin
Gardner. Bramhall House, 1960.
"The Immortal Game." Poul Anderson. *Pawn to Infinity.* Ace
Books, 1982, pages 57–70.
"The Royal Game." Stefan Zweig. *Woman's Home Companion,* Vol.
71, March 1944, pages 22–23, 96–98, 100–102, 106–111, 114–
115. Also reprinted in *The Chess Reader.* Greenburg, 1949.

Chess in Life

"The Problem of Paul Morphy." Ernest Jones. *Essays in Applied Psychoanalysis,* Vol. 1, 1951, pages 135–164. Also reprinted in *The Chess Reader.* Greenburg, 1949.
The Psychology of the Chess Player. Reuben Fine. Dover Publications, 1967.

Sam Loyd

Sam Loyd and His Chess Problems. Alain C. White. Dover Publications, 1962.
Mathematics, Magic and Mystery. Martin Gardner. Dover Publications, 1956.
Mathematical Puzzles of Sam Loyd. Martin Gardner, editor. Dover Publications, 1959.
More Mathematical Puzzles of Sam Loyd. Martin Gardner, editor. Dover Publications, 1960.

Riddles

A Book of Puzzlements. Herbert Kohl. Schocken Books, 1981.
1800 Riddles, Enigmas and Conundrums. Darwin A. Hindman. Dover Publications, 1963.

Magic Squares

The Wonders of Magic Squares. Jim Moran. Vintage Books, 1982.
Madachy's Mathematical Recreations. Joseph S. Madachy. Dover Publications, 1966.
Magic Squares and Cubes. W. S. Andrews. Dover Publications, 1960.
Mathematical Recreations and Essays. W. W. Rousse Ball. Macmillan, 1960.
"Magic Squares: A Design Source." Ben F. Laposky. *Leonardo,* Vol. 2, pages 207–209.

Nonsense Verse

The Limerick. G. Legman. Bell Publishing, 1969.

The First Clerihews. E. Clerihew Bentley. Oxford University Press, 1982.

Out On a Limerick. Bennett Cerf. Harper & Row, 1960.